HUNTING GHOSTS

A TEAM REAPER THRILLER
THE CABAL BOOK 3

BRENT TOWNS

WOLFPACK
PUBLISHING
— EST 2013 —

WOLFPACK
PUBLISHING
— EST 2013 —

Published in the United States by Wolfpack Publishing, Las Vegas

Wolfpack Publishing
5130 S. Fort Apache Road, 215-380
Las Vegas, NV 89148

wolfpackpublishing.com

Paperback ISBN: 978-1-64734-733-8
eBook ISBN: 978-1-64734-640-9

HUNTING GHOSTS

*For Sheila Nolan, proof that tough women
like tough books.
And as always, for Sam and Jacob*

PROLOGUE

Mosul, Iraq, 2016

Attired to blend with every other Muslim male in the city, Raymond "Knocker" Jensen's beard contributed to his overall appearance, under the guise of a native. The solid-looking SAS sergeant from 22 Squadron was, however, a far cry from being local. Hand-picked for the mission to Mosul, the seat of ISIS in the north of Iraq, the big man was there with one thing in mind: to assassinate a Jihadi named English Eddie, the man responsible for more than fifteen beheadings within the past four months. Two of that count had been British reporters; another a British SAS soldier lost in a raid while advising Iraqi soldiers.

With those deaths at the forefront of Knocker's thoughts, a grim determination that the bastard's days—correction, hours—were numbered overcame the wily Brit.

After insertion by a helicopter the previous evening some five miles from the city, Knocker had proceeded on foot into the hotbed of chaos, the ISIS stronghold, under the cover of darkness. He was armed only with a Glock 19 and his personal combat knife, and both weapons were concealed beneath his clothing. Now the wait began, watching for confirmation that his target was on-site.

"Mother, this is Scalpel, over," Knocker murmured into his comms.

"Read you loud and clear, Scalpel," a woman's voice replied in his ear.

"I need a sitrep, Mother. I've got at least three gentlemen here starting to take an interest in me, over."

"Sitrep is still the same, Scalpel," Ellen Grayson replied.

"For fuck's sake," Knocker growled. "I'm sitting out here like a honeymooner's dick. Find out where this cock is, or I'm pulling the pin."

"Hold your position, Scalpel. That's an order."

"Your order is fucked."

"The UAV is reading three heat signatures in the house opposite where you are, Scalpel. We think the target is one of them, but we need confirmation."

"Is the team on standby, Mother?"

"They're holding in the desert six klicks out, Scalpel. Once you have confirmation and terminate the subject, they will come and get you."

"Oh, shit," Knocker mumbled.

"What is it?"

"One of those cocks has decided to come over for a chat."

"Then get rid of him."

"How do you propose I do that, Mother? I'm in the middle of a fucking city where every second fighting-age male is armed with a bloody AK. I do something stupid, and the bastards will cut off my frigging head and put it on a pole." The hissed retort conveyed his frustration with the situation.

"Work it out, Knocker. That's why you were chosen."

"Fine, I'll work it out."

With the distance between them closing, the man addressed him briefly. Getting no response from Knocker, the man frowned, and the tone of his voice changed, becoming more insistent. That was the point when the SAS man knew he was in trouble. He said in a low voice, "Mother, Scalpel."

"Go ahead, Scalpel."

"Get that fucking team in the air now."

Realizing that the barely audible utterances were in English, the man stopped dead, frozen momentarily, providing Knocker with the edge he needed. The Glock came up, and he shot the man in the chest.

"What are you doing, Scalpel?"

Knocker started to walk forward and said, "I'm getting your sodding confirmation."

On the other side of the street, two men, startled

by the sudden eruption of gunfire, swung their weapons around to shoot the SAS man. Due to his superior training, Knocker shot them both before they brought their guns to bear.

As he walked past them, he bent down, picked up an AK, and kicked the door open. It slammed back, and Knocker walked inside.

Vauxhall, London

Ellen Grayson was seething. She'd worked day and night to put this op together, and it appeared as though a damned rogue operator was going to stuff it up royally. *Not on my watch.* "What the hell is he up to?" she hissed.

Shrugging his shoulders, the man seated at the console beside her said, "Looks like he's breaching, ma'am."

"I can bloody see that!" she snapped.

"Will I alert the team?" the man asked.

"Not yet. It seems that he wants to screw this op up, so I think he should be made to deal with the shit he causes."

The man looked up at her, concerned. "Ma'am?"

"You heard me, Rogers. Leave him there."

"Yes, ma'am."

"Colonel?" a fair-haired console operator from

across the room called to her.

"What is it?"

"We've got at least seven tangos starting to move toward the building."

"Understood."

Grayson stared at the split screens before her. One showed the immediate vicinity outside the target house, the next a heat map of the building. A third screen cast a wider net around the area, while a fourth was linked to the backup SAS team and the helicopter.

"Where is that bastard?" she growled.

"He's gone inside, ma'am."

"Christ. What about the targets?"

"Two are moving to meet him. The third seems to be seated," Rogers explained. He frowned. "Ma'am, the third guy isn't moving. I'm zooming in."

The heat signature grew larger, but for a moment, Grayson wasn't sure what she was looking at. It finally came to her. The person was seated, more than likely tied to a chair. "Shit. Get the fucking helicopter up *now*."

Mosul, Iraq

The inside of the house was sparsely furnished. Mostly it had mats on a dirt floor as well as a couple of chairs. Stacked in the corner of the first room Knocker entered were half a dozen AKs, two RPG launchers, some rocket-propelled grenades, and what looked to be body armor.

He hurriedly swept the room before starting for a doorway in front of him. He'd taken two steps when an urgent voice said into his comms, "Two tangos coming at you, Scalpel."

They burst through the doorway, both armed. Knocker fired the AK he had picked up and watched as both would-be killers fell to the floor.

Without hesitation, he stepped over them and into the next room. It was clear.

"Scalpel, this is Mother."

"Go ahead."

"There should be a doorway to your right. Do you see it?"

"I see it."

"There is an unknown inside that room. They look to be a hostage, copy?"

"Yes, ma'am."

Showing some caution, Knocker stepped into the room, sweeping it briefly before turning his attention to the figure in the chair. It was a well-lit space, with a single bulb hanging from the dirty ceiling. Dressed in filthy rage, the man beneath the light sat slumped over. Knocker hurried to him and, grabbing a handful of hair, lifted his face to the light so he could get a better look.

The man had been knocked about over some time, the dried blood, old bruises, and crusted scabs testament to the torture he had withstood. He was filthy and unshaven, and Knocker dug into his pocket to get his encrypted cell. "Who are you, cock?" he asked.

The man stared at him as though he were an apparition. He blinked when the flash of the cell's camera almost blinded him but remained silent.

"Come on, mate, tell me who you are," Knocker said as he untied the man's arms and checked them for identifying marks.

As he slid up the sleeve of the flaccid right arm, he found a tattoo. He froze and stared at the man's face again, trying to get a closer look. "Mother, this is Scalpel, over."

"Go ahead."

"Ma'am, looks like we've got one of ours here."

"Say again, Scalpel."

"This guy is SBS. From the looks of him, he's been in captivity for a long time. I've just sent you a picture."

"Did you get a name?" Grayson asked as the picture flashed onto a large screen in front of her.

"No, ma'am," Knocker replied.

"Is there any sign of the target, Scalpel?"

"No, ma'am."

Rogers said, "Scalpel, you're about to get visitors real soon. You've got tangos converging on your position."

"What's the ETA on the evac?"

"Ten mikes."

"Jesus Christ," Knocker snarled. "What the fuck happened?"

"We'll discuss it later," Grayson interrupted. "In the meantime, you need to hold the fort, as they say, until help arrives."

"Great." Knocker groaned and signed off.

He looked at the man before him. "I don't know if you can understand me, mate, but I need to get ready for the party. Wait here."

Knocker did a quick recon of the rear of the house but found no entries. "Thank God for small mercies."

Making his way to the front of the building, he took off his robes along the way, revealing the pants and T-Shirt he wore beneath. He grabbed a vest from the corner stack, placed it over his head, and secured it before moving to the front door, where he glanced each way along the street.

"Mother, what's the update on the tangos?" A burst of gunfire erupted, and bullets hissed and snapped all around the SAS man. "Shit. Disregard my last, Mother."

He ducked back into the relative safety of the house and waited for the firing to drop off, then opened up with his own weapon. He broke cover and fired at one man who was standing in the middle of the street. The man dropped and hadn't even stopped moving before Knocker was looking for another target.

More gunfire came his way, smashing chunks out of the external wall. The SAS man returned fire once more, swearing when the slide stayed back, indicating he'd run out of ammo. Throwing the AK on the floor, Knocker hurried across to grab one from the pile in the corner. He slid the slide back to check it, cursing once more. Hurriedly going through the rest of the piled weapons, he checked each but came up with the same result. "Of all the useless fucking... great bloody terrorists you lot are. I guess there's only one thing for it."

He picked up an RPG launcher and some grenades and headed for the doorway.

———————

Vauxhall, London

"Ma'am, I have an ID on the prisoner," a thin woman in a black blouse and skirt called to Grayson from her workstation.

"Don't keep me hanging, Harris," Grayson said curtly.

"Lieutenant Dan Best went missing a little over twelve months ago when the SBS raided a pirate camp on the Somali coast. Their team was looking for prisoners at the time and liberated six but lost one of their own. He just vanished. Once the team rescued the hostages, they went back to search for Best. They were on the ground for a week but failed to find any trace."

"And here he is," Grayson said.

"Yes, ma'am."

"Inform RM Poole we've found their man."

"Yes, ma'am."

A large explosion registered on the screen, drawing the attention of everyone in the room. "What was that?" Grayson asked.

"An explosion," Rogers replied.

"Yes, but what blew up?"

Rogers said into his comms. "Scalpel, sitrep, over."

"I'm still alive if that's what you're worried about," Knocker said. "But if that evac doesn't happen soon, I might as well kiss my ass goodbye."

"It's coming, Scalpel."

"So is fucking Christmas," Knocker said drily.

"Hang in there, Knocker."

Mosul, Iraq

Knocker fired another rocket-propelled grenade across the street at a building where two shooters had taken up position. One tango had a light machine gun and was laying down heavy fire. The SAS man was at risk of being pinned down while others assaulted his position.

The explosive streaked across the short distance and exploded with a roar. A large hole appeared in the side of the building, and dust and debris were strewn everywhere. The objective, however, was achieved since the machine gun fell silent.

Loading another grenade, Knocker prepared himself mentally for his next move. The dust was starting to clear, but a fusillade of bullets winged their way toward his position. He waited until there was a brief lull, then fired again. This time his target was a vehicle farther down the street. It was a white Landcruiser that provided scant cover for the two shooters who had taken shelter there.

The impact was devastating. The vehicle blew, engulfed in an orange fireball. One of the shooters, his clothes aflame, staggered screaming into the street before finally collapsing to the ground.

Knocker was preparing to reload when his comms crackled to life. "Scalpel, this is Black Knight One-One. Copy?"

Knocker frowned. The callsign for the Chinook was Chicken Hawk Three-Two. "Copy, Black Knight. Good to hear your voice, mate."

"We're about to do a sweep over your location. Keep your head down, over."

"Roger, Black Knight. Ready when you are."

At first, he heard nothing of the approaching

machine, then the *whop-whop* of the rotor blades increased in volume. A few moments later, dust and debris began swirling, and the street outside lit up as an M230 chain gun ripped it apart. Knocker smiled. Someone had scraped up an Apache attack helicopter for support.

The helicopter roared low, the rotor wash continuing to whip up the street's grit. The pilot pulled up and put distance between himself and his target before turning his aircraft around.

"Scalpel? Black Knight. Over."

"Copy, Black Knight."

"We're about to hit these buggers hard for you. Make them think again."

"What do you have in mind?" Knocker asked.

"We've got a Hellfire, which should knock a few of them arse over bollocks for you."

"Ready when you are," Knocker replied.

"Roger. Black Knight cleared hot."

Knocker hurriedly made his way back through the house to the room where he'd left the prisoner. The man was now lying on his side with his knees drawn up to his chest. The SAS man knelt beside him. "Hang in there, cock. The cavalry is on the way."

The man looked at Knocker for the first time, acknowledging he was there. "Who are you?"

"I'm the git who's getting you out of here," Knocker told him. "Just keep—"

There was a tremendous explosion outside as a

Hellfire from the Apache exploded a block down the street. The noise died, and Knocker spoke again. "Can you walk, mate?"

The prisoner shook his head. "No. My feet."

Knocker nodded and moved to look. "What's your name?"

"Lieutenant Dan Best. SBS."

The SAS man looked at Best's feet and saw the horrible scars just above his heels. The SBS man said, "I tried to escape a month after I was captured. The bastards cut my Achilles tendons on both sides."

"Shit," Knocker said, climbing to his feet. "Don't go anywhere."

"As if."

Knocker moved back to the front room and said into his comms, "Chicken Hawk Three-Two, copy?"

"Read you, Scalpel."

"ETA?"

"We're almost there, but there's a problem, Scalpel," the pilot informed him.

"You'd better not be giving me bad news, Chicken Hawk."

"I'm sorry, Knocker, but there is no clear LZ for at least a couple of blocks. You're going to have to DIY to the landing zone."

"Fuck!" Knocker exclaimed vehemently.

"Wait one, Chicken Hawk," the SAS man replied. "Mother, this is Scalpel."

"Go ahead, Scalpel."

"Ma'am, the prisoner is non-ambulatory. I need that fucking Chinook to put down on target."

"What do you mean, non-ambulatory, Scalpel?"

"I mean, the bastards crippled him, and he can't walk."

"Wait one, Scalpel. We'll assess the situation from here. Standby."

———————

Vauxhall London

"What do we have that's close?" Grayson asked Rogers.

"You heard the pilot of the Chinook, ma'am. There is nothing closer."

"There must be something. Find it."

Rogers began scanning the satellite feed they were hooked into while Grayson watched the feed on the screens. The street containing the target house was starting to resemble a war zone.

Smoke drifted skyward from various fires, and the heat signatures of gathering terrorists were appearing everywhere. If Jensen didn't get out of there soon, he'd be overrun. "Scalpel, this is Mother, over."

"Copy, Mother."

"You need to get out of there now."

"Repeat your last, Mother."

"You heard me, Knocker. Get the hell out of there. We can't get to you if you stay there."

"I'm not sure what you're suggesting, Mother. Did you say to get out? Over."

"You damn well know I did, Scalpel."

"And what am I meant to do about our friend, Mother? Please advise."

Keenly aware of the scrutiny of Rogers as well as several others who were listening in on the feed, Grayson said, "Confirm he's non-ambulatory, Scalpel."

"Affirmative, Mother."

"You'll have to leave him behind, Scalpel."

Silence.

"Confirm my last transmission, Scalpel," Grayson's voice was granite.

Her orders were confirmed when Knocker's voice came back over the comms. "Fuck you, Mother."

***

Mosul, Iraq

Knocker hurried over to the doorway and looked out. He was livid, not only at the issued order but because he could see no way around it. For the moment everything seemed to be clear, but he held no illusions that it would remain that way for long. The pall of black smoke drifting across the street offered good cover, but he needed to go now.

The SAS man hurried back inside. He crouched by Best and said, "The helicopter can't touch down here, so I'm going to have to carry you out."

"How far?" Best asked.

"A couple of blocks. Not far at all."

"You can't do that," Best said. "You won't make it twenty meters before they drop you."

"I guess we're about to find out," Knocker told him.

"What did your boss say?"

"What?"

"Come on, cock. You were never here for me. You were after that other dobber. The one that's been cutting the heads off hostages like me."

Knocker's expression gave it away. "Sorry, Best."

"Just do one thing before you go," the SBS man said. "Don't leave me alive for that bastard to cut my head off for the world to see."

"Shit!"

"Do it. You and I know it's the only way."

"Mother, this is Scalpel. Tell me you found something."

"Situation is still the same, Scalpel. Get out now."

"Fucking bollocks." The pressure of the situation caused momentary indecision.

"Do it, mate. You have to."

Knocker rose to his feet. Best fixed his gaze on him. Knocker felt numerous emotions rising within him: guilt, regret, anger. "Don't look at me, damn it."

Best dropped his gaze, and Knocker raised his Glock. He almost choked on the words as they came out. "I'm sorry."

———

"Mother, I'm moving."

"Roger, Scalpel."

Knocker had his Glock up and ready as he exited the house.

"Scalpel," Rogers said into his ear, "you need to turn right and make your way to the alley behind the building. Be careful. ISR shows a tango taking shelter there."

"Copy," Knocker said in a low voice.

He moved swiftly and turned into the alley, taking the shooter by surprise. The SAS man shot him at close range, pushing him out of the way as he fell.

"Right," Rogers said in a calm voice. "Once you reach the end of the alley, turn left and walk for one block. At that point, the street is clear."

"Roger."

Following the directions, Knocker turned left onto the dusty street. Behind him, farther down the thoroughfare, a vehicle with armed men in the back of it roared across an intersection. Knocker ignored its passage, relying on the intelligence in his ear and keeping his eyes focused on what lay ahead.

"Scalpel, once you reach the next intersection, turn right."

After acknowledging the instruction, Knocker followed it when he reached the turn. Halfway along the street, however, Rogers spoke urgently in his ear, "Danger close, Scalpel. Danger close. You have three tangos about to turn onto your street."

Remaining calm, Knocker glanced about, searching for a place to take cover. He noticed something suitable across the street.

Jogging over to the recessed doorway, he took shelter inside, controlling his breathing while waiting. Listening to their excited voices approach, Knocker frowned. They were speaking English.

"Mother," he whispered, "can I have confirmation that these guys play for the other team?"

"What's wrong, Scalpel?"

"They're speaking fucking English."

After a brief period of silence, he heard, "Scalpel, you are clear to engage."

Stepping out of the doorway, Knocker shot the first man twice in the chest. His aim shifted, and he repeated his actions for a similar outcome. Both men fell silently to the ground, their weapons leaving their hands. The third man dropped his weapon and threw his hands above shoulder height, calling, "Don't shoot!"

"I don't have time for this shit," Knocker muttered. "Who the fuck are you?"

"Tom. Tom Wiltshire."

"Where you from, Smeg?"

"Bournemouth."

"You should have stayed there. Turn around and start walking. You do anything stupid, I'll put one in the back of your head."

The young man started walking along the street. In his earpiece, Knocker heard, "What are you doing, Scalpel?"

It was Grayson.

"Bringing home a prisoner, Mother."

"Put a bullet in his head and get out of there."

"You're breaking up, ma'am."

"That's an order, Jensen," Grayson growled.

"Fuck you."

"Knocker, damn it—"

"Scalpel, out."

They continued along the street, and once they reached the intersection, Rogers said, "Turn left. Halfway along the street is a large square where the helicopter can put down. Good luck."

Knocker heard a distant helicopter on approach, the sound quickly growing louder. He said into his comms. "Chicken Hawk Three-Two, copy?"

"Roger, Scalpel."

"I'm about one mike out from the LZ, over."

"Roger, Scalpel. We'll see you there."

Knocker pushed the young man along in front

of him. "Where are you taking me?"

"Back to where you belong," Knocker told him. "Keep moving."

Reaching the square, Knocker pushed the young man to his knees to wait. "Chicken Hawk, we're on-site. Northeast corner of the square, over."

"Roger. We'll be there in three…two…one—"

The Chinook appeared above them with a loud roar. Dust violently kicked up from the square as the rotor wash stirred it. Knocker grabbed his young prisoner, hauled him to his feet, and shoved him toward the back ramp of the Chinook just as it touched down.

They were almost there when the young man stumbled and fell. Knocker tried to get him up, but he wouldn't respond. He rolled him over and saw the patch of blood on his chest. He'd been shot.

The SAS man looked at the top of the helicopter's ramp and saw one of the two SAS snipers standing there, his rifle cradled in his arms.

"Bastard," he hissed. "Fucking bastard."

Knocker ran the rest of the way to the helicopter and up the ramp and didn't stop until he'd crashed into the SAS operator. He felt the Chinook lift and bank to the left, but at that point, he didn't care. He was too busy beating the shit out of the shooter for killing his prisoner.

———————

It took a further twelve months for an SAS hunter-killer team to nail the Jihadi dubbed English Eddie. Twelve solid months of sifting through thousands of pages of intel and keeping agents on the ground. After the assassination attempt in Mosul, he just disappeared. Then a thread appeared, one mentioning an Englishman and Mogadishu.

British Intelligence investigated and came up with two pictures. Both were of a heavily bearded man who always wore sunglasses and robes.

Soon after that, they got lucky. A third photo was snapped, this one showing a partially exposed right forearm with a portion of a tattoo. English Eddie had tattoos, three of them. One on his right forearm. The intelligence guys analyzed the shit out of the thing until they were almost certain the man they had recently dubbed Tatt Man was indeed English Eddie.

Hereford was on standby, and within twenty-four hours, a six-man team from 22 SAS Squadron was in the air.

Dropped on target with aircover on standby should it be required, the mission went off without a hitch. The team was extracted with the DNA evidence needed to identify the dead terrorist.

Two years after that, in 2019, another terrorist rose to the top of the most-wanted list. The intelligence community was calling him The Ghost. No

one had seen him, hence there were no pictures on
record. Rumor had it that he was a Westerner, but
no one could prove it. The only proof they did have
was the pile of bodies that continued to climb. Jour-
nalists, aid volunteers, military personnel, civilian
contractors. Even prominent politicians.

His movements were tracked from Africa to
Europe and Iraq. Once, he was even in Syria. By
the time any Western intelligence agencies got a lead
on him, he was gone. The Ghost certainly lived up
to his name.

Then it all changed.

CHAPTER 1

"Oh, motherfu—"

"You okay, Knocker?" John "Reaper" Kane asked the former SAS man as he writhed in pain on the floor.

"She kneed me in the bloody bollocks, Reaper," he moaned, gasping for breath.

"Perhaps you shouldn't have tried your British charm on her," Kane opined with a grin.

Knocker looked up into the face of the Team Reaper leader. Kane was a solidly built man who stood six-four and had short black hair. His nickname originated from the large tattoo of the Grim Reaper on his back. Reaper leaned down and put a hand out for Knocker to take. "Here."

He dragged the former SAS man to his feet and

said, "You look a little green."

Knocker breathed deeply, composing himself, then said, "Give me another beer and I'll wash it away."

"Did I miss all the fun?" Cara Billings asked as she approached their table, placing their beers on cardboard coasters. Once a Marine Corp lieutenant as well as a deputy sheriff, she now was the Team Reaper second in command, armorer, and sniper.

In her mid-thirties, she worked out daily to maintain her slim, muscular figure in peak condition.

Kane laughed. "Knocker tried one of his never-fail British pickup lines and got kneed in his balls."

Cara smiled.

"It's not bloody funny," Knocker said. "It hurts."

"You need someone to rub it better for you?" Cara suggested jovially.

"Are you volunteering?"

She held up both hands. "No. You never know what I might catch. That thing of yours is probably as bad as Axe's."

"Ease up," he said indignantly. "Nothing is that bad."

She nodded. "You're right. I apologize."

"Speaking of our illustrious comrade," Kane said, "have you seen him?"

Knocker nodded toward the corner of the room where the tall, bearded former Recon Marine sniper stood talking to a couple of ladies. "Looks like he's working on his next tattoo."

"Don't say that," Kane said with a shake of his head. "Don't even think it. You know what he's like."

"I see Axe is working on his next tattoo," Richard "Brick" Peters said as he joined them.

Kane glared at the former Navy SEAL with the shaved head and said, "Don't you frigging start."

Brick rubbed his beard. "What did I say?"

"Reaper's just jealous that Axe is getting his Bell End in more than him," Knocker replied.

Cara looked at him incredulously. "That's a new one. Why haven't I heard that before?"

"Because I'm a gentleman."

"And you're full of shit." Cara laughed as she took a sip of beer, then licked froth from her top lip.

"I'm hurt," said Kane, taking a pull of his own drink.

Brick looked at Axe and his lady friends. "You want I should go over there and give him something to knock him out?"

Brick was the team's combat medic and a damn fine one. His skills had been called into action on more than one occasion.

Kane shook his head. "Not yet. But if he starts toward the door with either one of those ladies, I'll knock the bastard out myself."

"Is Axe working on his next tattoo?" a female voice asked, causing those around the table to erupt in laughter. Everyone, that is, except for Kane.

General Mary Thurston looked confused. "Did I miss something?"

Cara smiled broadly. "No, ma'am. Not yet anyway."

Kane stared at the commander of the Worldwide Drug Initiative. For a woman in her early forties, she looked mighty good. Her long dark hair, normally worn tied back, was loose today. It hung past her shoulders, accentuating her face and brown eyes. Apart from Cara, she was one of the most aerobically fit in the organization.

"Can I get you a beer, ma'am?" Brick asked.

Thurston shook her head. "I'm here to see Knocker, actually. Luis said you were all here winding down from the training exercise today."

"What did I do now?"

She smiled at him. "Nothing. However, you and I are flying to Virginia tomorrow for a meeting with the CIA director."

"Do we know why?" he inquired.

"No, we don't know why."

"I'm not sure if that's good or bad."

Thurston's face was deadpan. "It can't be good."

"You're right."

"Don't look now, but Casanova is coming this way with some arm candy," Brick said out of the corner of his mouth.

They all turned to glance at the couple heading in their direction. Axe was grinning from ear to ear, while the dark-haired lady on his arm appeared to be apprehensive.

"Hey, everyone," Axe said. "I'd...whoops! Hi, General."

"Axel."

Axe glanced at Kane. "Did I do something wrong?"

"Not to my knowledge."

"Whew. When she called me Axel, I thought for a moment I might have fu...I mean, stuffed up." He shot an apologetic look at his companion.

"Nope."

"I'm right here, Axel," Thurston said. "You know that, yes?"

Axe gave her a big grin. "Yes, ma'am. And looking splendid, as always."

"Are you taking the lady to Bedfordshire or the tattoo parlor?" Knocker asked.

Kane gave Knocker a perplexed stare.

Axe shot him a what-the-fuck look, but his lady friend spoke up. "No, he's not taking me to bed, and I know nothing about any tattoo parlor."

Her accent was heavy. Knocker smiled. "West Country?"

She nodded.

Axe smiled. "She talks better than you do, ya git. And she's a doctor."

Cara reached across the table. "I'm Cara. Take no notice of these apes."

"Gwen,"

"I'm Mary," Thurston said, introducing herself.

"You're the Iron Lady," Gwen said.

Thurston looked at Axe, who dropped his gaze and cleared his throat. "Anyone want a beer?"

"Where are you a doctor, Gwen?" Thurston asked, not taking her eyes off Axe.

"I'm at El Paso Municipal. I work in the ER."

Knocker threw back the last of his beer and said, "I'd love to stay, but apparently I have a plane to catch in the morning, so it's time for me to skive off. Nice to have met you, Gwen. Just be aware the big guy is a bit of a poser."

Gwen's smile broadened. "You're no friend."

He winked at her. "Goodnight, everyone."

Thurston said, "Don't be late, Knocker. I'm not coming around to your place to drag you naked out of bed."

"You been looking through my window again, General?" He laughed as he turned away.

"Get out of here."

———

The air outside was cooling rapidly, and the night was expected to be quite chilly. The parking lot was reasonably well-lit, but there were shadowy patches throughout it.

Knocker pushed the door open and walked

down the concrete steps and out into the lot. Gravel crunched beneath his boots as he moved in the direction of his truck, which was parked at the far end.

He stopped, leaning his head to the left as he squinted to sharpen his eyesight and focused on the shadow lurking by his vehicle. "Oi, scouser, what the fuck you think you're doing?"

A man stepped into the open, the streetlamp bathing him in light. "Hey, Knocker. Long time no see."

The former SAS man frowned. He could see the face and knew it, but from where? Then it came to him. Mosul, Iraq. He was the SAS sniper who'd killed the kid, that he'd crash-tackled on the Chinook. "What do you want?" Knocker asked, unable to remember his name.

"Is that the way to greet an old friend?"

"We aren't friends, cock. Never were."

The man shrugged. "Oh, well, I guess you're still the same daft cow you were then."

Alarms were going off in Knocker's head. Something was wrong, and the situation had a stench like week-old roadkill. He reached behind his back and wrapped his hand around the butt of his SIG Sauer M17.

There was movement to Knocker's right, and a second man emerged. So, this was their game; it was an ambush. "Whatever you blokes have planned, you might want to think again."

"We were told to say hello before we killed you," the first man said.

Knocker frowned. "By who?"

"The Ghost."

"The Ghost?" Knocker asked, confused. "The crazy fucker all the intelligence agencies are chasing? That Ghost?"

"That's him."

"Well, stuff me. Old Knocker's become famous."

The M17 came out from behind Knocker's back and fired twice. Both rounds hit the first man in the chest, killing him instantly. The man on Knocker's right started to bring his gun up into a firing position, but the former SAS man was still on edge from the training that afternoon, and his movements were fast and fluid.

The next two shots blew one hole in the man's chest and another in his throat. He went down clutching the spurting wound, trying to stanch the flow.

Keeping his handgun centered on the shooter who was still alive, Knocker strode forward. He stood over the dying man and shot him again. Threat neutralized.

Going through their pockets, he found a motel key and two Texas driver's licenses—no doubt fakes. Both men had died armed with Glock 19s.

A crowd began to gather, and next he knew, Kane and Thurston were beside him. "What happened?"

the general asked.

"These two knobs tried to ambush me."

Gwen pushed her way through the gathering crush and went to the first man. Knocker said, "You're wasting your time."

She ignored him and checked anyway.

The rest of the team arrived and began moving the onlookers back, preparing some space for the inevitable arrival of the police. Kane said, "You know these guys, Knocker?"

He nodded. "One of them. From Mosul. But that was a lifetime ago."

"Why would they want to kill you?" Thurston asked.

"I don't know, ma'am," he replied, leaving out the piece of information about The Ghost.

"Get your story straight," Thurston said. "It looks like it'll be a long night."

_____

Langley, Virginia

"I swear, I'll never get used to driving this damned desk," CIA Director Alex Joseph growled.

"You've been in the job five minutes, Joe," General Hank Jones said to his friend. "Give it time."

Both men had been career armed services until recently. Alex Joseph had been appointed Director of the Central Intelligence Agency after the last one to hold the position was terminated with extreme prejudice. Hank Jones, on the other hand, was Chairman of the Joint Chiefs.

"All this damned paperwork, Hank. Drives me up the damn wall."

"It's no more than what you were doing before, Joe. Run with it. The President made a good choice when she picked you."

"We'll see," the gray-haired director said.

Jones sat in a large chair across the desk from his friend. He had served in Vietnam back in the day as a member of the 75th Rangers. A big man in his late sixties, many people who saw him thought he was a Norman Schwarzkopf Jr. look-alike.

"Care to tell me what the meeting is about, Joe?" Jones asked.

"I will fill you in when Mary arrives."

About to say more, the general stopped and turned to look as the door opened and Thurston and Knocker entered. "Sorry we're late, Admiral. Traffic was a bitch."

"You can drop the 'admiral' bullshit, Mary. I'm not that man anymore. As the job reminds me every day."

"Yes, sir." She looked at Jones. "General."

"Hello, Mary. You're looking well."

"Feeling good, sir."

Joseph stared at Knocker. "What about you,

son? Recovered?"

"Ready and willing, sir."

"We'll see. Take a seat, and we'll get started."

Joseph fingered a folder that sat on the hardwood desk in front of him. He stared at Knocker and said, "I asked for you, Jensen, because of your experience."

"Yes, sir."

"I need a man to go into Mosul. It has to be someone I can trust. The mission is making contact with an agent we have there who has been monitoring a very small pocket of Jihadists who may be starting a recruitment drive."

"Why can't you just bring him out?" Knocker asked.

"Because he is part of the cell. He managed to get recruited and is now embedded with them."

Knocker stared at him curiously and shook his head. "No, there's something else. Something you're not telling me."

Joseph opened the folder and slid a picture across the desk. "This is our man. We've not heard from him in over a week."

"A week?" Knocker asked, raising his eyebrows. "I'm sorry, Admiral, but he's fucked. If he's been dark for a week, then it's all over. We might as well head back to HQ now."

Thurston put a hand on Knocker's arm. "Just hear him out, Ray."

"All right."

"It may well be that his cover has been blown and they've taken him out. We can't be sure. What we do know is that he was close to giving us an ID on a high-value target."

"Which HVT might that be?" Knocker asked.

"The Ghost."

Knocker's blood ran cold. Had the occurrence of the previous night been a coincidence? He shook his head. "Before you go any further, there's something you should know."

———————

Once he had related the story, Thurston clenched her jaw and said, "We'll talk about this later."

The look on her face told him she was angry, and frankly, he didn't blame her. "Yes, ma'am."

"You say you knew one of the shooters?" Jones asked, speaking for the first time since the briefing had started.

Knocker nodded. "We had a history."

"What kind of history?"

"The kind that saw me punch the shit out of him."

"I see."

"So, it wasn't a grudge that was behind it, then?" Joseph asked.

"No, sir. He mentioned that The Ghost said to say hello."

"It would seem The Ghost knows you, or of

you, leastways," Jones said. "Someone you pissed off, maybe?"

"I have pissed a lot of people off over the years," Knocker said. "On both sides of the fence."

"Anyone specific spring to mind?"

"No, sir."

Joseph's stare hardened. "This is the closest we've been to this madman in a long while, Jensen. Will you do it?"

Knocker thought for a while before he answered. "Yes, sir. I'll go. I'm guessing I'll not have any backup while I'm there?"

"Help will be over two hundred miles away, son. If you need it, however, you'll have a number to call. Just don't expect it to be there at the drop of a hat."

Thurston said, "Don't feel like you have to do this, Knocker."

She gazed at the other men. Joseph nodded. "The choice is yours. This is not an order. If you don't want to do it, just say no."

"I'll go, sir. Ma'am. This guy came after me, and I want to find out why."

CHAPTER 2

Shali, Chechnya

The two DEA operatives were hiding in a rundown building on a debris-strewn third floor that overlooked the meeting place. Intelligence said their target was meeting a second party at four that afternoon. Mike Brand looked at his watch and muttered a low curse. "This ain't happening today, Chuck. It's almost five."

Lying beside him, dark-haired Chuck Tyler kept the binoculars trained on the target area as though they were glued to his eyes. "Patience, Mike, patience."

"We've been in position for hours." The fair-haired Brand was not known for his patience.

"We'll give it another thirty minutes and then pack up," Tyler told his partner. "How's that sound?"

"All right."

Before ten minutes had passed, they had movement.

The first to arrive was a dark Range Rover with such deep tint on the windows that it was impossible to make out whoever was inside. It pulled into the parking lot of the abandoned factory opposite and just sat there idling and waiting. Then came a Mercedes. Like the Range Rover, every glass surface was dark. It too stopped in the lot, opposite the other vehicle.

Doors opened, and four people alighted from each. Six of those were armed and set up a small perimeter around the other two. "Get some pictures, Mike," Tyler said to his partner.

Brand was ahead of that curve, and the pictures were starting to flow.

Tyler focused on the two primary targets below. One they already knew: Kenji Ishida, head of the Ishida-gumi Yakuza syndicate. While not the largest in Japan, it was one of the fastest growing.

The two DEA men weren't sure about the identity of the other new arrival. She was female; the headscarf and shapely figure gave that away. The dark glasses helped conceal her identity. Brand took numerous pictures of her so the analysts could check their computers with the latest facial recognition software to figure out who she was.

The two talked for a moment before turning to their men, sending them to their vehicles for different reasons. The woman approached Ishida and shook hands with him, then they turned to watch Ishida's man return with what looked like a compact notebook computer. He set it on the hood of the Mercedes and typed something. Ishida and the woman watched, and once it was complete, she turned back to her man.

"I guess that was the money transaction," Tyler said. "Now for the drugs."

"Why would the head of a Yakuza syndicate be buying drugs, Chuck? He supplies the shit all over the world."

The answer became clear when it was dragged from the rear seat of the Range Rover.

"Shit," Tyler hissed. "Make sure you get this."

A hooded figure was shoved toward the Yakuza boss, then the hood was removed to reveal a man of Asian descent. The prisoner blinked when he saw who was standing before him. In that short space of time, Kenji Ishida drew a handgun and placed it against the prisoner's head. The woman stepped aside, and Ishida pulled the trigger.

"Fuck," Tyler growled. "Tell me you got that."

"I got it," Brand said in a low voice. "But somebody sure screwed up. This was supposed to be a drug exchange."

"Let's get out of here. We need to find out who that woman is."

Worldwide Drug Initiative, El Paso, Texas

When Thurston got back to the WDI HQ, she called Kane and Luis Ferrero into her office to explain what was happening. Kane wasn't thrilled about being an operator down with the possibility of an operation starting but he'd deal with it.

Ferrero took it in his stride. The former DEA agent, who was in his late forties, was the man who'd put the original team together. Then Thurston was installed in the position, leaving Ferrero in charge of operations.

"Do we know how long he will be gone?" Ferrero asked.

"No idea," Thurston replied.

"I suppose we can run operations with a four-person team. Wouldn't be the first time."

"Good," the general said. "I'm glad you feel that way because something came across my desk I think might need looking into."

She pushed a folder across her worksurface toward Ferrero, who leaned down and flicked it open. The first page was a picture of Kenji Ishida. Ferrero looked questioningly at Thurston.

She said, "There is a picture below it."

Ferrero moved the picture and saw another of a woman. It was grainy, but it was unmistakably a female. "Who is she?"

"We don't know."

"You want us to find out?"

"Yes."

"Why?"

Kane reached out and moved around some of the items in the folder. He came across two more photos. One was of a man being taken from the back of a Range Rover. The other was of Ishida shooting him.

Thurston said, "The DEA had people on the ground surveilling Kenji because there was a rumor of a big drug deal going down. Instead, this was what they witnessed."

"Where were these taken, ma'am?" Kane asked.

"In Chechnya."

"The guy Kenji shot must have been mighty important for him to travel that distance to get there."

"Or the woman who handed him over doesn't like traveling," Ferrero theorized.

"Who is the guy?" Kane asked.

"Ryuu Kita," Thurston supplied. "Finding that out was easy. He disappeared two years ago with a million of Yakuza money. He was formerly Kenji Ishida's accountant."

"No wonder he put his lights out. You don't cross the Yakuza and get away with it."

Thurston nodded. "I had Slick do some digging for me. I called him from the plane just after I left Washington. Kenji did indeed fly out from Japan for the meeting. The woman, on the other hand, is a ghost."

"There's a lot of that going around lately," Kane muttered.

"Slick tried to track her using satellites that were in the area, along with anything else that could give us a picture of her movements but came up empty-handed."

Ferrero frowned. "Nothing? The guy is an electronic genius, and he has nothing?"

"The satellite feed was jammed, same with everything else. It was all down for an hour."

"I still find it hard to believe Slick came up empty-handed," Ferrero said.

"Intelligence agency background?" Kane asked.

"It's possible," Thurston said. "However, I've still got Slick digging around the dark side, trying to find something."

"What do you want us to do?" Kane asked Thurston.

"You've got the easy job."

Kane grimaced. "Whatever you're about to hand us, I'm sure it'll be anything but."

"Let's say there's a good chance we'll kill two birds with one stone."

Both men stared at her, waiting for her to elaborate.

"You'll abduct Kenji Ishida so he can be questioned, and in the meantime, with a little luck, he'll give us information on the woman."

"Where are we supposed to grab him from?"

"That's the best part. Break out the longboards, Reaper. You're off to Hawaii."

"Gather around," Kane said, looking at his team.

As the team members moved closer, they stared at him in anticipation. "We're about to go operational."

"What shithole this time?" Axe asked.

"You'll like this one, Axe," Kane said with a grin. "We're headed to Hawaii."

The operator's mouth split into a huge smile. "Sun, sand, and babes. My kind of shithole."

Cara elbowed him in the ribs. "What happened to the good doctor, Casanova?"

Axe eyed her as though she was stupid, and he shouldn't need to explain the situation. "I'm still seeing her. Doesn't mean I can't look, though."

"We going one man down?" Brick asked, glancing at Cara. "Sorry, ma'am."

Kane said, "Knocker is otherwise occupied doing something for the CIA."

"Do we know what?"

"Need to know."

"What are we doing in Hawaii, Reaper?" Cara asked, bringing the focus back to their op.

"Kenji Ishida. We're going to abduct him for

the DEA."

"Wow, going after a Yakuza boss! That's next-level."

Standing silently among them was a person who hadn't spoken since hearing about the mission. Kane looked at Carlos Arenas. A former member of the assault team, the one-time Mexican Special Forces commander was now their mission planner. His experience was unrivaled. "What say you, Carlos?"

He nodded slowly. "It can be done. A lot of planning will be needed."

"Something you're good at."

Carlos began speaking slowly as if he were thinking out loud. "He'll need to be grabbed and taken off the island the same day. Preferably within an hour of him being taken."

"We can do that."

"The hardest part will be not knowing his itinerary."

Kane smiled. "That's the beauty of it. We don't need to. We know where he's staying."

"Get me the details, and I'll have something for you by the time we land."

"You're coming?"

"*Amigo*, someone has to make sure you stay out of trouble."

"All right, then. Let's get everything organized. We leave tomorrow. Cara, a word."

As the others left, Cara walked over to Kane.

"What's up?"

"This thing with Knocker has me troubled. He's out there on his own, and no one wants to read us in."

"He's a big boy. He can take care of himself."

Looking her in the eye, Kane asked, "Do you still have your friend at Langley?"

Cara shook her head. "Reaper, don't—"

"I need to know what he's into."

"Shit. All right, I'll make a call. I'll come to your place tonight if I come up with anything."

"Thanks."

———————

Sam "Slick" Swift sat staring at his computer screen, unwilling to admit defeat. His eyes were burning from hours of looking at the monitor without a break. He'd searched and searched but found nothing to get him excited. He ran a hand through his red hair and let out a long sigh. Muttering something under his breath, he began typing again.

There was movement beside him, and a voice said, "How's it going, baby?"

He looked up at Brooke Reynolds. He saw the large coffee in her hand and asked, "Is that for me?"

"Sure is."

Reynolds was the commander of Bravo element. Most of their work was behind the scenes. The lithe woman was a qualified UAV pilot as well as an occasional field operative. Her long black hair was tied back in a ponytail, and she wore tank top and sweatpants. Swift took the coffee. "Thanks. You been working out?"

"Yeah. Trying to get rid of the pent-up energy being non-operational leaves me feeling."

"You need to find yourself a guy," Swift told her.

She smiled. "I wish. You've still got nothing, I gather?"

"Not a damned thing. It's like she's a ghost. There one minute, gone the next."

"Did you try running facials on her bodyguards?"

He nodded. "Nothing."

"Were there any reports filed in any countries about kidnappings?"

"I went back a week and came up empty. I had to use tight search parameters, though. If I hadn't, the results would have been a nightmare."

Reynolds stared at the picture for a long moment. "I'm sorry, Slick, but I'm done. If only there was something you could use to identify her. Something that isn't her face."

Swift's eyes widened, and he jumped to his feet. "Yes!"

Reynolds took a step back as he whirled around. "What?"

"You're magnificent," he told her excitedly, putting the coffee on his desk and slopping some on the surface. He cupped Reynolds' face in both hands and kissed her. "Absolutely magnificent."

Surprised by the behavior of the normally self-controlled computer tech, she asked, "What did I say?"

"Look at the picture. Her hand. What do you see?"

"Fingers?"

"Look closer."

"She's wearing some kind of ring."

"Exactly. If I can work out where it was made or which store it came from, I might get somewhere."

Reynolds nodded. "Glad to be of help."

Swift sat back down and started working once again, this time with more vigor. "Sorry, Brooke, I need to get back to this."

"Never mind me. I need to shower anyway. Just let me know if I can help."

Without looking around, he said, "You already have. You already have."

"Don't you ever lock your door?" Cara asked as she walked into Kane's living room.

He looked at her and shook his head. "Nope. I figure if they want me bad enough, a locked door ain't going to help any."

"An open one is just an invitation."

He reached under a cushion on the sofa and

pulled out his M17. "I always keep a little deterrent handy. You want a beer?"

"Sure, why not?"

"They're in the refrigerator. Grab me one while you're there."

"Asshole."

She came back with a couple of beers and sat on the sofa next to Kane. He screwed the top off his and took a long pull. It tasted even better than the last one. "What did you find out?"

Cara stared at him for a moment, contemplating her words, then took a drink of her beer. She said, "Here's an idea. Instead of talking about classified shit, let's have sex. It'll probably be safer."

He chuckled. "As good as that sounds, I'll take the intel."

"All right." She sighed. "But you really have to sit on this, or my friend could get reamed seven different ways."

"Cross my heart."

"The admiral has sent Knocker to Mosul in Iraq. Something to do with them being close to finding The Ghost."

Kane sat forward. "On his own?"

She nodded. "Uh-huh. He's been there before. An agent has gone off the grid, and Knocker's supposed to make contact with him. Apparently, the guy infiltrated a cell and suddenly disappeared."

"Shit. They should never have sent him alone."

He took another pull of his beer.

"Oh, that's not all. It gets better. Those guys who tried to kill Knocker the other night? They told him The Ghost said to say hello."

"You're shitting me!"

"Nope."

"Remind me to talk to him about what it means to be part of a team."

"Uh-huh."

"Is that all?" Kane asked.

Cara took another drink and nodded. "Pretty much."

"Is everything squared away for tomorrow?"

"Sure is."

"I guess you'll be going home, then."

She smiled around the bottle. "Eventually."

He cocked an eyebrow. "Eventually?"

She crept on hands and knees across the sofa until she was straddling his thighs. "Yes, eventually."

———

Swift's eyes widened. "Yes! Yes! Yes!"

He'd done it. He had found out where the woman purchased the ring. Exploding out of his chair, he began dancing around it like a cheap stripper. Hips gyrating and thrusting and—

"Is this a private dance, or can anyone join in?" Thurston asked.

"Holy crap!" Swift blurted and regained control of himself. "I thought everyone had gone."

"Obviously," Thurston said. "Why the…whatever that was?" She pointed up and down with her right index finger.

"I found out where the woman bought her ring."

She gave him a weird look. "All right."

"The woman from the picture. The ghost woman."

"Oh, right."

"She bought it from a specialized jeweler in Europe," he told her. "In Geneva, Switzerland."

"You're sure?"

"Yes, ma'am."

"Is there any footage of her at the store?"

"I'll try to find some, but this is all I have at the moment."

Thurston nodded. "That's good work, Slick. Now, go home."

Exhaustion swamped him, and he realized that many hours staring at a screen took its toll. "You know what, General? I might just do that."

He grabbed his coat from the back of his chair and started toward the door. "Goodnight, ma'am."

"Goodnight," she called after him. Then, "Slick?"

He turned. "Yes, ma'am?"

"The dance. Never again, got it?"

He smiled sheepishly. "Got it."

CHAPTER 3

Mosul, Iraq

Mosul was a mess. When the Iraqi and Coalition forces retook the city from ISIL, large portions were destroyed. Knocker hadn't seen devastation like that since the team had been in Aleppo six months before. Buildings had bullet and shell holes, and some were just blown into rubble.

Dressed like a local in a thawb and a keffiyeh, Knocker moved down the debris-strewn street. His face was unshaven, and his M17 was hidden beneath his garments.

He'd been in Iraq for all of twenty-four hours, Mosul, even less. The transport he'd been given was parked a block away, a Toyota Landcruiser. Hidden in the back of the vehicle, beneath the floor was an M4A1, magazines, a vest, and a second encrypted cell, along with a couple of extra passports and press

IDs saying he was a freelance reporter for the BBC.

Although Mosul had been virtually cleared of ISIL extremists, there were still some there, people who had been able to escape the net and joined up with smaller terrorist groups. One of those, the CIA's man in Iraq had been able to infiltrate.

Knocker stopped, aware that some of the civilians were staring at him. He ignored them and cast his gaze on the building across the street. This was supposed to be where the CIA's man, Abbas, lived.

A local stopped and stared at him. He had a long black beard and angry eyes. He stepped toward Knocker and said in Arabic, "*Min 'anat?*" *Who are you?*

Knocker glared at him. "I'm no one you need to concern yourself about."

Over the past few years, the former SAS man had brushed up on his Arabic, so he spoke it well.

"What are you doing here?" the man asked.

"Why do you want to know?"

"I have not seen you here before."

"And after today, you probably won't again."

"Who are you?" the man asked again.

"Go away."

"No, I will not go," the man said defiantly. "You do not belong here. It is you who should go."

Knocker sighed heavily, then reached inside his thawb and took out the M17. "Fuck off."

The man backed away. At first, he was intimidated by the weapon and the sudden outburst in English. Then his face screwed up in anger, and he spat on the ground. "Go, or your bones will bleach under the hot sun."

A crowd was starting to gather, drawn by the commotion. That was the last thing he wanted. "Shit."

Knocker glared at the man once more and started to walk away. Behind him, the man spat on the street once more and hurled insults at his back.

He disappeared into an alley and stopped, waiting for the man to move on. Eventually, the man did.

After several minutes, Knocker went back, but this time he went to the door of the house instead. He knocked and waited.

A woman answered. Not old, early thirties. She looked at him and said almost timidly, "Yes?"

"I'm here to see Abbas."

"He's not home."

She started to close the door, and Knocker braced his hand against it. "I'm a friend of his."

"My husband doesn't have any friends."

Knocker changed to English. "Can I come in?"

Alarm showed on her face. "No, go away."

"Listen, I need to talk. If I stay out here, people will get curious. They will want to know who I am."

She opened the door wider. "Come."

He entered and stopped inside the door. Closing it behind him, she then began to lead him farther into her home. Knocker said, "Here will do. I don't want to intrude."

She nodded tentatively. "Okay."

"Can you tell me where Abbas is?"

"I do not know."

"How long has he been gone?"

"Two weeks."

Knocker winced. Two weeks was a long time, and if he had to put money on it, he would guess that the man was dead. "What is your name?"

"Akira."

"Akira?"

"Yes. What is your name?"

"Call me Ray."

"Ray."

"Akira, where did Abbas go?"

"I don't know."

Knocker was getting nowhere. "Did he say anything?"

She shook her head. "I am worried."

"You should be. Do you know if he kept anything here?"

Akira stared at him, still unsure whether to trust him. Knocker said, "I'm here to help. You can trust me."

She guided him into what passed for a living room and stopped. Shoving aside a coffee table, she then pulled a rug back to reveal a trapdoor. With a low grunt, she opened it and exposed steps leading down into the earth. "Follow me."

Descending the steps took them into total darkness. When she reached the bottom, Akira turned on a small light to reveal a hidden room that might have been in some kind of spy movie.

There were maps on the walls and a locked cabinet that might have contained guns. Pictures. Knocker walked over to them. "Are these the men from the cell?"

"Yes."

"I suppose you wouldn't know where they hang out?"

"There is a building near the market," she said.

Knocker turned his head slowly to stare at her. At first, he wasn't sure he'd heard it, but it was there. "You're American."

"Yes, I was born there and brought up in New York. So was Abbas."

"I did not see that coming. Did the cell know Abbas grew up in America?"

"I don't know."

"I want you to think about this very hard, Akira," Knocker said firmly. "Has Abbas been acting any different? Could he have gone to the dark side?"

She looked at him in disbelief. "This is not a *Star Wars* movie."

"Think. Has he been acting any different?"

"Maybe a little, but it doesn't mean what you think. He was starting to believe that he might have been compromised."

"Why didn't he get out, then?"

"He couldn't. It was too far along."

Knocker nodded. "The Ghost?"

"Yes," she said. "He was close. Really close."

"Nothing is too close," Knocker told her.

"Even if he'd seen the man you are all hunting?"

Knocker was stunned. "He's seen The Ghost?"

"Yes."

"Does he have a picture?"

Akira shook her head. "No. However, he said that he walks funny."

"What did he mean, 'funny'?"

"I do not know."

Knocker had to relax, bring his heart rate down. No one—no intelligence agency—had ever been this close. He focused on the pictures stuck to the wall. There were four of them, and each had a name: Ahmad, Latif, Jakeem, and Hadi. "And you said these men are from the cell?"

"Yes. They are part of a bigger organization. There are a lot of smaller cells broken up throughout the city. Only the ones in the cell know who their members are. No one knows those who are in the other cells."

"Makes sense. How did he get to see The Ghost?"

"I don't know."

Knocker nodded. "Thank you for your help. I'll go to the market and see what I can find out."

Akira walked over to a drawer and opened it.
The former SAS man noticed a remarkable change
in her demeanor. She reached inside the drawer
and took out a handgun. From where he stood, it
was hard to make out what it was. Like a skilled
professional, Akira dropped out the magazine and
checked it, then slid it back home. She racked a
round into the chamber and hid the weapon below
her garments. "I'm sick of waiting and doing nothing. I'm coming with you."

Knocker nodded. "I guess you are."

—————

The market was busy, but that helped the couple
blend in better. Armed militia still roamed the
streets, but luckily, they showed no interest in them.
Knocker had parked his ride a block away.

Akira nodded at a bullet-pocked building behind
a dried meat stall. "That one there."

Knocker shifted his gaze. It was two stories tall
and had a small balcony with an armed guard on it.
"That doesn't look too good."

"He is always there."

"Is there a back way in?" Knocker asked.

"I don't know."

"Let's have a look."

They walked away from the market and found
an alley that led them to a back street which, like

many others, was littered with trash. Knocker turned into it and walked parallel to the direction they'd come. When he figured he was in the right place, he stopped. It did have a rear entry. They studied the back of the building, looking for cameras or other security devices. A man appeared, stern-looking with a thick beard. "What do you want?" he growled. "Go away."

Knocker looked at the AK he held. The former SAS man raised a hand and started to walk away with Akira.

"Wait," the man said. "Turn around."

Knocker stopped and turned, as did Akira. The man peered at her and said, "I know you."

She nodded. "Yes."

"What are you doing here?"

"I'm looking for my husband."

"He does not want to see you anymore. Forget you ever knew him."

"But he's my husband," she replied.

"Not anymore. He is one of us. He will soon be joining the martyrs who have gone before him."

Akira looked shocked. "What?"

"Go away."

"No. Tell me about my husband."

The man started to bring up his AK. Knocker grabbed Akira's hand, mindful of propriety, and turned her away from him. He said quietly. "Not now, Akira. Let's go."

"He's my husband. I want to know—"

"Move before you get both of us killed," he whispered harshly.

Akira kept walking, and Knocker glanced back. The man continued watching them as they moved up the alley before finally turning to go back inside. The couple stopped, and the former SAS man said, "I'll come back tonight."

"What if something happens before then?" Akira asked.

"It won't. Trust me."

When Knocker returned that evening, he had the M4 as well as the vest. Moving stealthily through the shadows until he reached the back door of the building, he paused. As far as he knew, there were five men inside. However, there might be more. What he wouldn't give for some darkness and a set of NVGs.

He'd left Akira with the vehicle up the street. Once the shooting started, she was to drive to the alley and wait for him to come out. If he took longer than ten minutes, she was to leave without him.

Knocker tried the door, which was locked. Shit, he'd have to go in hard. Having studied a picture of Abbas until the image was burned into his brain, he took a deep breath and kicked the door open.

It crashed back with a loud bang. Knocker had the M4A1 carbine at his shoulder in the firing position. He had no sooner entered when the first shooter appeared. Knocker fired twice, and the man sat down hard without firing a shot. Shouts echoed throughout the building as the startled terrorists began running around, gathering themselves.

Knocker moved past a staircase into another room toward the front of the building. There he found another shooter, who he put down quickly. The man did not fire a shot before Knocker killed him.

Hearing footsteps tromping down the stairs behind him, he whirled to fire but wasn't fast enough. Instead, he was forced to dive into the room in which he'd just killed the second shooter to avoid a hail of bullets.

Knocker grunted as he hit the hard-packed floor, then rolled onto his back and sat halfway up with bullets ricocheting around him. Catching sight of the shooter, he fired his weapon. Three down.

Knocker scrambled to his feet and swiftly moved to the base of the stairs. He aimed the carbine upward and waited for several seconds in case another shooter was coming down them, but he was clear.

The former SAS man began moving up the stairs, his actions as fluid as water. Reaching the rough landing at the top, he almost walked into a storm of 7.62 rounds. He fired reflexively, his years of training and muscle memory providing the aim.

The M4 rattled noisily, and the shooter jerked violently under the impact of each shot. His arms flung out wide, and he squeezed the trigger involuntarily. Bullets punched into the wall as he fell.

The count was four down, but not one of them was Abbas.

Knocker moved slower now. There was no telling what he might find. There were three rooms upstairs; he cleared the first two and went to the third. "Abbas, are you there?"

There was a drawn-out silence, then, "I'm in here."

"Come on out. I'm here to take you home."

"Home where?"

"Back to the US. But we have to leave now."

There was a moment more of silence before Abbas appeared. "We'd better go then."

"Yes."

Knocker led the way down the stairs and had almost reached the bottom when he sensed rather than saw the danger. He threw himself to the floor, twisting as he went and bringing up the M4. A handgun cracked and the bullet tugged at his pants leg, missing the flesh. The former SAS man fired, and the bullet took Abbas in the chest.

The CIA man fell forward and landed in a heap at the bottom of the stairs. "Shit!" Knocker scrambled forward.

Abbas was still breathing but wouldn't last long. "Why?" Knocker asked savagely.

"The...The Ghost was right."

"The Ghost? Where is he?"

"Gone."

"Damn it, Abbas. What about Akira? What about your damn country?"

"This is...is my country."

"Where is he? The Ghost, where?"

Abbas coughed. It was wet. "He knew your people would come, so he left."

"My people? You work for the CIA—"

Abbas shook his head vigorously. "No. We do not. Not anymore."

Knocker thought for a moment before something troublesome occurred to him. "You said—"

Abbas was dead.

"You killed him," Akira stated.

Knocker stood and turned to face the woman, who had her handgun trained on him. "You too, huh? I should have figured it out sooner, but—"

"The Ghost is a great warrior. He will unite the kingdoms and lead us forward as one against the infidels."

"He's a bloody murderer."

"He will lead the martyrs into battle against our enemies and to the ultimate victory."

"Fuck it," Knocker said and shot her.

———————

Knocker carried her into her home and dropped her on the floor. Akira let out a yelp as her wounded leg sent bolts of pain through her. She scrambled away from him as he checked the flesh wound in his arm from where she'd shot him after he'd fired. He grunted and walked over to her, took a handful of hair, and dragged her to the center of the room.

The former SAS man let her go, and she slumped. She looked up at Knocker and spat in his direction. "Listen," he said. "The only reason you're still alive is that I don't particularly want to kill you, understand? But don't push your luck."

"Do it!" she snarled.

"What I don't get is why you didn't betray me earlier?"

She said nothing.

Knocker reached into his pocket and took out an encrypted phone. He punched in a number, and a voice answered, "Slick speaking."

"Slick, it's Knocker. I need a favor. Are you at work?"

"Shit, Knocker! I'm at my desk."

"Don't let on it's me—"

"You know these things are recorded, right?"

"They are?"

"Yes."

"Fuck. You need to find one from a week ago where I called a number in Waco."

"What? Why?"

"I was talking to some cow I met at a bar—"

"I don't want to know."

"She was a good shag."

Slick sighed. "Knocker, what do you need?"

"I'm going to send you an address in Mosul, Iraq. I want you to look for any feed you can find of a man with a funny walk leaving the building there anywhere in the past two…no, three weeks."

"Why?"

"I can't tell you. I need you to trust me on this one, mate. It's to do with what I'm working on."

"All right, I'll see what I can come up with."

"Thanks, you're a good chap. How's the rest of the team?"

"They've flown to Hawaii."

"Lucky bastards. They get all the fun. Don't forget about that call I made."

"I'll fix it. Now, let me get to work."

Knocker disconnected and made another call. After a few minutes, the call was rerouted to its destination.

"Joseph."

"Admiral, I've got news. And you're not going to like it."

CHAPTER 4

Sunset Sands Hotel, Honolulu, Hawaii

"I could really get used to this gig, Reaper," Axe said as he watched two ladies walk past him, wearing string bikinis and walnut-colored tans. "Yes, sir, I really could."

"Just keep your eyes on the prize, Reaper Four," Cara said from the other side of the crystal-clear pool.

"I never took them off it, ma'am."

Kane grinned. He could imagine Cara rolling her eyes about now. "I must say, ma'am," Axe continued, "you certainly fill out a bikini yourself."

"Keep it up, Axe, and I'll smash this wine glass and come over there and stab you in the eye with the stem."

Brick interrupted their banter. "All right, people, game faces on. I've got our target coming out now."

"Does he have girls with him?" Axe asked.

"As a matter of fact, he does," Brick said. "And three bodyguards."

"I call shotgun on the ladies," Axe said with a grin.

"Careful, Casanova," Thurston said over the comms from the ops room in El Paso. "I'll lay good money on them being fighters."

Kane sat up on his sun lounge. He watched the small procession walk around the far side of the pool and take up residence at two tables they pushed together and said into his comms, "Reaper Five, go."

"On it."

"Hey, Reaper, I think one of those gals just winked at me."

"Axe, don't even move...oh, shit. What the fuck are you doing?"

Nothing says trouble like a bearded, six-foot-and change, grinning buffoon with tattoos, dressed in flowery swimming trunks. Kane heard him say through the comms. "Gents, ladies. How are we today?"

One of the big bodyguards stood up and approached Axe. He said something in Japanese and waited.

"What the hell is he doing, Reaper?" Cara asked.

"I really have no idea."

"All right, I'll go and rescue him before he screws this up," Cara sighed.

"Please do."

Cara got to her feet and walked in the direction of the Yakuza boss and his entourage. "You know what?" Kane said. "You really do look good in that red bikini."

"Bite me."

As she reached them, Kane heard her say, "What are you doing?"

Axe mumbled something, and Cara stepped closer to him and gave him a shove. "What did you say, asshole? Were you flirting with these bitches?"

Axe said, "What if I was?" Cara shoved him hard enough to make him stagger and fall toward Ishida. The Yakuza boss put his hands up to stop him from landing on top of him. He spoke savagely to Axe, something about cutting his balls off if he didn't go away. Axe apologized and walked away. Cara slapped him up the back of the head as he went.

"What the fuck was that, Axe?" Kane growled.

"If you would ask our tech guru to switch his frequency, you'll find out that I just bugged our friend over there."

"Stupid," Kane growled in a low voice.

"Maybe, but we might get something."

"Slick, did you get that?"

"Already on it, Reaper."

"Cara?" Kane said.

"Yes, Reaper?"

"Hit the asshole again."

"With pleasure."

Brick's job was to get eyes and ears inside the suites booked by Ishida and his group. He took an elevator to the fifteenth floor, got off, and turned left, heading along the hallway to the end door that led into the suite.

"Slick, I'm here."

"All right, wait one."

After a few seconds, the electronic door lock beeped, and its guts made the snapping sound that indicated the door was open. Brick drew his suppressed M17 and eased into the room, closing the door behind him.

The first thing he did was sweep the suite for hidden surprises. Then he took out his cell, which Swift had worked on before he left. After three minutes, Brick had located three hidden cameras and two mics. "Slick, did you get the frequencies?"

"All good, Reaper Five. I can use the cameras and mics, but maybe place a camera of our own and a mic somewhere, over."

"Copy that."

That took another two minutes.

"Reaper Five, copy?"

"Copy, Bravo."

Thurston said, "Have a look around and see if you can find anything that might be useful."

"Roger that."

He started in the main bedroom, looking through drawers, being careful to place everything back where it was found. Then came the luggage, and again, everything went back exactly. "I've got nothing," Brick said as he walked back out into the main living area.

"All right, Reaper Five, get out."

Brick started toward the door, then stopped. "Bravo, copy?"

"What's up, Reaper Five?"

"Ishida killed his old accountant, which means he has a new one. Now, if I had an accountant that turned on me, I wouldn't want to be letting the next one—"

"—out of my sight," Thurston finished for him. "Which means that one of his entourage is most likely his new accountant."

"My thoughts exactly, ma'am."

"Get out of that room, Reaper Five, and wait for my instructions. There are four more rooms on that floor booked by Ishida. Stand by."

"Bravo to all Reaper call signs. We believe that one of the entourages is an accountant. We believe it is one of the three ladies."

Kane looked at the three women in their bikinis.

Two were dressed in white, one in black. He raised his cell and took a photo. "Ma'am, I'm sending you a picture of the one I believe fits the bill."

"That was quick," Cara said.

"Three women, one wears a black bikini, the other two are in white. The one in black has a bodyguard glancing at her with a monotonous regularity like he's either got a hard-on for her or she's under his special watch."

"Stand by."

A minute later, Ferrero came back over the comms. "Reaper, it looks like you were right. Her name is Heidi Fuchida."

"Did you say, 'Heidi', Zero?"

"Affirmative, Reaper. Her mother was American and her father was Japanese. Keep an eye on them; the mission has just evolved."

"Make it evolve faster, Zero," Cara said. "It looks like our little bird is leaving. And her bodyguard is going with her."

———

"Reaper Five, you need to pick it up," Thurston said.

"Pick it up? I just got in here, ma'am."

"She's on her way back with company."

"Understood."

Brick swept the room and found another camera and a mic, which Slick attended to while the former

SEAL started sifting through anything that might be helpful. Once more, he checked drawers and luggage but came up with nothing. "Slick, how do accountants do everything these days?"

"Electronically, my web-footed friend."

Scanning the room, Brick said, "So, we're doing this all wrong. I should be looking for something small. Something—"

After a period of silence, Swift said, "What is it?"

"I might have something."

It was a small figurine of a Chinese dragon. "Why would you have that?"

"Brick, you need to pick it up faster," Thurston said with urgency. "They're in the elevator. Forget it and get out."

Brick ignored her and picked up the figurine. He shook it gently and heard the rattle. "Bingo."

"What are you doing, Brick?" Kane asked.

"I'm onto something."

"Get out, damn it. You heard the general."

There was a small door in the bottom of the statue. Brick opened it, and out came a small thumb drive. "I've got it…I think."

"Got what?"

"I'm not sure."

"Put it back and get out."

"What if it's important?"

"What if she finds it gone?"

Brick reached into his pocket and took out the

contents—a few dimes and a pack of gum. He broke it in half and placed it into the statue, then closed the door and shook it. Sounded almost the same.

"All right, I'm—" The door snicked as the electronic latch opened, "Too late."

Brick headed for the balcony, went out the sliding door, and slipped around the corner out of sight. Unless she came out, there was no way she could see him.

"Brick, are you good?" Kane asked impatiently.

"For the moment."

He peered around the corner and saw the woman looking around the room. It was almost as though she could sense that someone had been in there. Brick saw her go over to the small statue and pick it up. She gave it a shake and replaced it, reassured.

Walking over to the bed, she began to undress. First off was the bikini top, then the bottom. Brick turned away before the bottom came off and waited until he could hear the water running in the shower before he spoke. "Bravo Four, talk to me."

"Her shadow is out in the hallway, Reaper Five. There's no going that way."

"What background do you have on her?"

"Name, Heidi Fuchida. She's a resident of Osaka. Father is native Japanese; her mother is American. She went to Harvard, sent there by her family. Studied business, and once she graduated, she returned to Japan. Worked with a couple of big firms, then for some reason, she went to work as an accountant for a company which was owned by Ishida."

"There's nothing stating why?"

"No."

"Can you do a quick search into her financial status?"

"Give me a minute."

"No rush. I've got all day."

"What are you thinking, Brick?" Kane asked.

"Maybe she's not working for him by choice."

"That's a big assumption, Reaper Five."

"She could be good for the DEA if she is, though."

"You there, Brick?" Swift came back to him.

"Copy."

"He's paying her fifty thousand a month."

Brick had to stop himself from emitting a low whistle.

"There is an anomaly, however," Swift informed him. "A portion of it is going to an account registered to her parents, the other into a different account which is virtually untouched."

"She's not spending it?"

"Nothing apart from a couple hundred here and there. Enough to live off, and that's it."

"What about an apartment?" Brick asked.

"Ishida owns it."

"How much is in the account?"

"A hair under a million and a half."

"She's taking money for her parents but not for

herself."

"That's about it," Swift confirmed.

"Reaper, copy?"

"I'm here," Kane replied.

"What are our friends up to down there?"

"Just enjoying the rays. Why?"

"I'm going to have a talk with Heidi."

"That's not advisable, Reaper Five."

"She might be our way in. If we can turn her to our side, then we can get Ishida's itinerary. It'll help us to get him, and she can form a case for the DEA."

"General, are you listening to this?" Kane asked.

"I'm here."

"What are your thoughts?"

"It's worth the risk."

"Ma'am, we're going to need to give her something," Brick told Thurston.

"What are you thinking?"

"Protection for her parents. Maybe get them on a plane to the US."

"If that's what it takes, I'll authorize it, Reaper Five."

"Thanks, ma'am."

He waited until she had showered and dressed before he acted. When she went into her bedroom, he entered the living room and hid beside the door. As she came out of the bedroom, his hand snaked out, and he clamped it over her mouth.

"Not a sound," Brick hissed into her ear. "I don't intend to harm you."

He could feel her screams against the palm of his hand. "Listen to me. Listen. Listen."

Heidi calmed down, breath replacing the muffled screams. "I'm going to take my hand away from your mouth and we're going to talk. Do you understand?"

She nodded.

"Before I do, know this. If you scream, your friend out in the hall will come barging in here, and I'm going to have to shoot him."

She nodded again.

"Are we good?"

Another nod.

Brick lowered his hand.

With her body against his, he could feel her top half expand as she drew a deep breath. Brick's hand moved back to her mouth before she could let it out in an ear-piercing screech. "No, no. Don't do that. I thought we had an agreement."

Heidi struggled against him but soon found out it was useless.

"Listen to me," he hissed angrily. "We know. Okay? We know you don't want to be here."

It was worth a shot, and it worked. She stopped squirming and relaxed.

"We're going to try again. Okay?"

She nodded.

Brick lowered his hand, and nothing happened.

He turned her around and looked into her eyes. There was a mix of fear and—

"*Daijobudesu ka?*" (Are you alright?) The voice came from the hallway.

Heidi stared at Brick, who was poised in case she screamed. Instead, she called in a calm voice, "*Daijobudesu.*"

She looked at Brick and said, "I told him I was fine."

He stared at her for a moment. With her long hair and fine features, she was quite pretty. "Thank you."

"Who are you?"

"I work for the American government."

"What do you want?"

"Kenji Ishida."

Heidi looked scared. "I can't help you."

"Yes, you can, Heidi."

"You know my name?"

"Yes. We also know about your parents and believe that Ishida is using them against you so you'll work for him."

She didn't need to answer; he could see it in her eyes. "We can help you. We can get them protection and out of Japan."

"How? How can you do that?"

"Trust me," Brick said. "We can do it."

"And what do I have to do in return?" Heidi asked.

"Help us with Ishida. Testify for the DEA—"

"No, I can't."

"Listen, Heidi. Do you know what happened to his last accountant? Do you?"

Her head bobbed. "I know."

"Were you there?"

"I was in the car."

"Who was the woman? The one that brought the package?" Brick asked.

Heidi shook her head. "I don't know. They call her Nemesis."

"Nemesis? As in the Greek Goddess?"

"Yes."

"Okay. Do you know anything else at all about her?"

"No. Except she is British."

"You're sure?"

"I heard her speak."

Brick nodded. "That's good. Now, do you want us to help you?"

She hesitated for several moments, contemplating the offer, then said, "Yes."

"Why is Ishida in Hawaii?"

"He has a deal happening," Heidi told him.

"When?"

"Tonight."

"Where?"

She shook her head. "I don't know."

"Can you find out?"

"I can try."

"I'll give you a number. You need to memorize it.

Get us the details and leave the rest to us. We'll have you out of this in no time."

"What about my parents?"

"As soon as you give me the details, we'll pick them up."

"Okay."

Brick dug into his pocket and took out the thumb drive. "I also have this."

"What? How?"

"I'm good at what I do. Now, I need to get out of here, and the only way I can do that is for you to take your friend out there for a walk. Will you do that?"

"Yes."

"Good. Get to it."

Kaneohe, Hawaii

The DEA had set the team up out of the way in Kaneohe. The house was large and practical, with an operations room full of everything they might need. While they waited, the team was debriefed, and every morsel of their intel was analyzed.

"What do we know?" Ferrero asked from the big screen.

"Not a lot," Brick said. "She'll reach out when she knows where the deal is going down. The intel from the thumb drive is in Slick's hands. However, she gave me a name for the woman who delivered the wayward accountant. You're not going to like it. She's called 'Nemesis'."

"Oh, that's just great," Slick said off-screen. "Just great."

"Care to share, Slick?" Ferrero asked.

He appeared on the monitor next to Ferrero. "Well, you all know what I'm about to say, right?"

Kane nodded. "Do it anyway."

"Nemesis was a Greek Goddess, the goddess of retribution. Which she showed by delivering the accountant to Kenji Ishida. Now it all seems to fit. It's amazing what a name can do. I managed to trace some of her footsteps by using her purchase of a ring in Geneva."

"So, you know who she is?" Kane asked.

"No."

"But you said—"

"I said I was able to trace some of her steps. I couldn't get enough for facial ID because she always changed her disguise. The one thing that remained the same was—"

"The ring," Cara finished.

"That's right. I've placed her in five cities across Europe in the past three months."

"Is there anything linking her to her visits there?" Kane asked.

"Now that I know those bits of intel, it'll give me

more to look for," Swift explained.

For a long moment, no one spoke. A pall of silence seemed to envelop both El Paso and Hawaii. It lasted thirty seconds, then Swift said, "Do I need to say it?"

"What?" Kane asked.

"Is anyone thinking Cabal here?"

"Nothing says Cabal, Slick," Kane replied.

"Really? How about Nemesis for a start? The woman is a ghost. She has access to things only the intelligence community has access to, and—"

"All right, Slick, we get the picture," Ferrero said. "Get me evidence."

"I'll do better than that, I'll find her, and you can ask her yourself."

He disappeared off-screen and left them to it. Ferrero sighed and was about to say something when Cara spoke. "What are the chances that he could be right, Luis?"

"Anything is possible. We never did find out who was accessing the accounts. Anyway. Keep me up to speed with the Ishida situation as it develops."

"Yes, sir," Kane said, and the screen went dark.

"Man, I wish those Cabal fuckers would crawl away and die already," Axe growled. "You know the shit is going to hit the fan if it's them, don't you? It's fucked up."

"Relax, Axe," Cara said to him. "It is only speculation at this stage. We have no idea if it's true."

"Ma'am, you know how our luck runs. If there's any likelihood it is true, we'll be up to our necks in assholes trying to kill us. Mark my words, this can only end badly."

Vilnius Lithuania

Nemesis sat on the hotel balcony enjoying her morning cup of tea. Below on the street, traffic was starting to build, both vehicular and pedestrian. In the room behind her, she heard the encrypted satellite phone ring. There were a few words uttered on her end, then a thin man appeared on the balcony behind her. She sighed. "What is it, Henry?"

"Your presence has been requested in Khartoum, ma'am," the man named Henry said in a heavy British accent. "A customer wants your services and is willing to pay a million dollars just for meeting with them to discuss it."

Nemesis placed her tea on the table and turned. "A million just to appear?"

"Yes, ma'am."

"It sounds like a trap to me," she said.

"I would have thought so too, ma'am, but for the name of the man who wants to meet with you."

"Oh?"

"Yes, ma'am. He's called The Ghost."

CHAPTER 5

Hawaii

Word came from Heidi later that afternoon. The meeting was to take place in Kalaeloa at an old refinery close to the docks. Ishida was meeting with the hierarchy of the H-41s, or Hawaiian 41s. They were an organized crime syndicate that ran most of the drugs on Oahu. All members had links to incarcerated ancestors from 1941 when the Japanese attacked Pearl harbor. If you weren't linked, you didn't get in.

Kane and the others geared up and moved into position early, their backup provided by the DEA field office. Swift had a good feed from an NSA satellite and could monitor everything from WDI HQ.

"Radio check," Kane said into his comms.

"Reaper Two, read you Lima Charlie."

"Reaper Four, read you Lima Charlie."

"Reaper Five, read you Lima Charlie."

"Zero is good."

There was a pause, then, "Pineapple Lead is good."

Kane shook his head. Damn Axe and his sense of humor. "Copy, comms are good."

Cara had secreted herself on top of an old oil tank, where she would have a clear field of fire with the M110A1 Compact Sniper System. She began sweeping said field, searching for anything that might remotely be construed as out of the ordinary. With that done, she radioed Kane that all was clear.

"Now it's a matter of patience, I guess," he said. "I hate waiting."

The wait wasn't as long as expected. "Reaper One? Bravo Four. We've got movement on ISR. Looks like three vehicles traveling at speed coming your way."

"Good copy, Bravo Four. Everyone, heads in the game."

A minute or so later, three black SUVs arrived on-site, forming a U-shape as they pulled up. Cara said, "Fancy."

"Gives them cover in case something goes wrong," Kane surmised. "My bet is that they're armored too."

The doors opened, and four bodyguards climbed out. They were all armed with SIG MPX Ks, compact weapons that carried a thirty-round magazine. Cara said, "Looks like they've come to play, Reaper."

"Home team can accommodate them," Kane said. "Bravo Four, any sign of the 41s?"

"They're coming in now, Reaper. Three sedans about to arrive on-site…wait one."

"What's up, Slick?"

"Ooh, these guys aren't playing by the rules. They've got a fourth vehicle coming in the back way. It's just pulled up outside an old warehouse to the north of the meeting place. I count five shooters climbing out and moving into position."

"Roger that, Bravo Four. Keep an eye on them." Kane took a moment to think. "All right, let's see how this plays out. Remember, Ishida is the package, and our mission is to keep him alive no matter what."

The three sedans arrived and disgorged their loads. Unlike the Yakuza, who were dressed in suits and looked like they were about to dine out at a fine restaurant, the 41s looked like street thugs in jeans and T-Shirts or tank tops. Most had multiple tattoos and wore gold jewelry of some description.

"Those assholes are fucking wannabe boys from the hood," Axe growled. "The Yakuza guys will eat them for supper."

"I guess that's why they brought the extra muscle."

A door on one of the SUVs opened, and Kenji Ishida climbed out. However, he wasn't alone. Heidi was with him. "Shit," Brick murmured though his comms. "What now, Reaper?"

"The plan remains the same. We just have to hope she keeps her head down once this thing kicks off."

"Reaper One, the extra shooters have moved into position," Swift informed them.

Cara swept the warehouse. "I've got them, Reaper. There is a bank of large windows that they're using as vantage points."

"Can you take them, Reaper Two?"

"On my worst day," she replied.

"Them first."

"Copy."

The two leaders walked toward each other with a single bodyguard each. After speaking for several moments, they returned to their vehicles, where they grabbed separate items. The Yakuza boss grabbed Heidi by the arm while his bodyguard took a briefcase. The leader of the 41s took out a struggling male who was dressed similar to them.

"What the hell is this, Reaper?" Brick asked.

"Slick, can you get a look at who the 41s are trading here?"

"Wait one, Reaper."

"Don't wait too fucking long. Slick," Brick said. "Shit is going down now."

Thirty seconds later, Swift said, "Reaper One, they are trading their leader."

"Holy shit. They're giving Ishida their boss to kill," Kane said. "But why...they're onto Heidi. Reaper Two, take out those extra shooters. Axe, the

41s are yours. The rest of us move in. Now."

Cara was already in action when they moved. The CSASS slammed back into her shoulder, and the first shooter hidden behind the glass of the warehouse died with a 7.62 round in his brain. With the sniper system, she was using the weapon in semi-automatic mode, which meant she could aim and fire without having to reload. So, while the first one was falling, there was a second bullet in the air, reaching out to terminate the next target.

On the ground, Axe had opened fire with the team's suppressed M249 light machine gun, while Kane, Brick, and the DEA agents closed on the rest of the armed men. The Yakuza shooters brought up their weapons and began to spray bullets wildly at their attackers. On the other hand, the professional-ism of the team and the DEA shone through as they carefully chose and eliminated targets. It took very little time for it to be all over, the outcome being that nearly all the bad guys were down. Then came a cry of, *"Medic!"*

Kane rushed over to where the cry had come from, but Brick had beaten him there. He looked down at the casualty and saw that it was Heidi. "Reaper One to Zero, over."

"Copy, Reaper One."

"We need a medevac in the air now. We've got a—"

"She's priority one, Reaper. She needs out now."

"Our WIA is a priority one, Zero. I say again,

priority one. Brick is doing all he can."

"Roger, Reaper. Priority one medevac."

Kane looked around. "Axe, secure the prisoners. Keep Ishida separated from the others."

"Roger that."

He missed having Knocker around. His extra muscle would have been good in this instance.

"Reaper One? Zero. Your medevac is in the air. ETA five minutes."

"Copy, Zero. Five minutes, out."

Kane looked down at Brick. The medic had an IV bag and tubing in his hands, but he didn't move as he looked down at his patient. "Ah, shit."

"Brick?"

"She's gone, Reaper. I couldn't help her."

Kane said, "You did your best."

"I did fuck-all."

Kane walked away from his friend and pressed the talk button on his comms. "Zero, this is Reaper One."

"Copy, Reaper One."

"Be advised, Zero, our WIA is now a KIA, over."

"Roger that. Out."

Cara appeared beside Kane. He glanced at her. "You want to give Brick a hand getting Heidi ready for transport?"

She nodded. "Yeah. I can do that. It's all mucked up, Reaper."

"Yeah, it is."

—————

Sudan, Outside Khartoum

Upon landing in the country, Nemesis followed the instructions she had been given. She crossed the Blue Nile and proceeded into the desert for fifty kilometers before reaching a mudbrick compound off the side of the road. Her escort consisted of six men, all specially trained and more than competent in their duties, armed with Heckler and Koch G36K compact assault rifles. The two armored SUVs stopped in a cloud of orange dust, and their drivers turned the motors off. The men climbed out first, forming a secure perimeter around the second vehicle.

After they were set, Nemesis climbed out of the rear passenger seat of the vehicle they stood guard around. She closed the door and looked about. "Dry bastard of a place this is."

"Reminds me of my missus' twat before we got divorced," one of the bodyguards said.

Nemesis glared at him. "Maybe because you're shit in bed, Collins. Or your neighbor was fucking her instead because you were a dud screw."

The others chuckled at the comment. One thing Nemesis had was a whip-like tongue that, when used effectively, cut deep.

The man named Collins scowled at her back.

Nemesis was dressed in a white suit, a wide-brimmed white hat, and dark sunglasses. There was a slight bulge outlined by her coat where her personal weapon, a Glock 19, sat in its shoulder holster.

"Well," she called, "where the fuck is everybody?"

There was movement from the doorway of the compound, and four men emerged. Three were armed with AK-47s, while the fourth held nothing. He stepped toward Nemesis.

Instantly six men raised their G36s and aimed at the threat. One of them said in his tell-tale British accent, "I'd stop there if I was you, old cock."

The man, who was dressed in a thawb, stopped and raised his hands. "I am no threat. We are here to welcome you to this meeting. Besides, if we wanted you dead, it would be so." He indicated the desert to their right, and through the heat haze, the visitors could see a line of armed men numbering around thirty.

Nemesis nodded. "All right. You've shown me yours, now I'll show you mine."

She raised her hand to shoulder level and waited. The snap of a high-powered round coming in was followed by a thud and the rolling report of the shot. One of the men who had emerged from the compound dropped where he stood, watched confusedly by his comrades. Nemesis said, "I also came prepared. I have two snipers out in the desert, as well as an assault team. After all, you never can be too careful."

"We were told you were careful. I am Amun. Come inside. He awaits you."

Nemesis stepped forward, followed by two of her men. Amun held up a hand. "Just you alone."

"Not on your life, mate," one of the men said. "Where she goes, we go."

Nemesis looked at the bodyguard. "It's fine, Mark."

Mark Miller was a former Royal Marine Commando and the head of Nemesis' personal detail. "Are you sure?"

"Yes."

Nemesis followed Amun into the compound. The interior was as barren as the never-ending miles of nothing outside the compound. Everything except a chair and a cane screen had been removed from the yard. "You will sit on the chair," Amun said.

Nemesis did as she was told and sat on the plastic chair. From behind the screen, a voice said, "Welcome to Sudan."

"I take it you're the one I'm here to meet?"

"I am. If you give Amun your account number, he will transfer the money you were offered for your attendance."

Nemesis reeled off the appropriate numbers and waited for the money to be transferred. Once the transaction was complete, Amun showed her the confirmation, and she nodded in satisfaction. With that done, she said, "Why have you summoned me here?"

"I have a job for you. I've been told that you are good at what you do."

"And I heard you were British. I guess our intelligence sources were accurate."

"I daresay they are."

"Who do you want me to do?"

"A British SAS man named Raymond Jensen. I want him brought to me. Alive."

"All right. I think I can manage that. Do you have any idea where he is?"

"The last I heard, he was in Mosul, Iraq. He may still be there. I do not know."

"Even if he isn't, it gives me a place to start. Killing him would probably be easier."

The Ghost considered. "My original order was for his death, but fine. If you can't bring him to me alive, I will accept his head."

"Original order? You've tried before?"

"Yes, but those who went before you were far from up to the task."

"Of course, there will be a price," Nemesis said.

"I will pay you ten million for the man. Five million for the head."

Nemesis thought about it for a moment before saying, "Agreed."

"Then our business here is concluded."

"Where do I make the delivery when I am done?"

"Amun will give you the details," The Ghost

told her. "Goodbye."

Nemesis left the barren compound and walked through the dust to the SUV, where Amun handed her a slip of paper with details for the delivery to The Ghost. The meeting concluded, the team loaded into their vehicles once more and headed back to Khartoum. As they left, Nemesis said into the lapel mic she had donned before the meeting, "Flint, remain in position and see what you can get me on that bastard."

"Copy, ma'am."

Royal Palms Hotel, Khartoum

Reclining in a lounge chair, Nemesis sat listening to the report former SAS sergeant Ben Flint, her head of operations, was giving. In her right hand was a photo, one of four her team had managed to get.

The suite she was in was large, bordering on palatial. Her bodyguards were staying on the same floor, while the operations team was rooming on a lower floor.

"That was taken twenty minutes after you left," Flint said. "He was picked up by a Land Rover, and they drove off."

While the picture was of good quality, there was no clear image of The Ghost's face. The only identifying features that might be useful were the crutches the man used. However, he wasn't called The Ghost for nothing. He would disappear like a grain of sand in the desert he drove into.

"I'm sorry, but we couldn't get a picture of his face."

Nemesis laid the photo on her lap. "Never mind. It was worth a try. Have our friend in Zurich look into it. Maybe he can come up with something."

"Do you really want to do this, ma'am? Looking into clients like this isn't something we usually do."

"We've never had a client with a fifty-million-dollar bounty on his head either," she pointed out.

CHAPTER 6

Mosul, Iraq

For two days, Knocker had been waiting for word from Swift—two long, boring days. He knew they were locked in on an op, but the guy was supposed to be shit-hot on a keyboard. It was with clipped tones that he answered the call when it came. "What the bloody hell have you been doing, mate?"

"You knew we had an op on, right?" Slick reminded him.

"Yeah, I knew that, but I've been in this shithole with my thumb up my ass for two days, waiting for you to call me back. Now, what do you have?"

"Nothing."

"Bullshit. You must have something."

"Nope, nothing. I'm sorry. The only way that guy you were asking about could get in and out was if he was a gopher."

It hit Knocker how he'd done it; there was a tunnel under the building. That meant he was going to have to go back.

"I'm sorry, Slick. Thanks for your help."

"I'm just sorry I couldn't help you any more than I have."

"No problem. Say hi to the others for me."

He disconnected and went into the other room of the safe house. There were two British Secret Intelligence Service agents going over papers at the table. He said, "I have to go out. I need a ride."

One of them, a woman he knew as Tracey, looked up and asked, "Where?"

"Back to the scene of the crime," Knocker told her with a smile.

"Are you crazy?" she asked.

"I think there is a tunnel under it."

"The place will be crawling with police, terrorists, even bloody Santa Claus."

"That's why I'll go after dark."

"What good is it if you find the tunnel anyway?" Tracey asked.

"I have a guy who can work wonders with a satellite. He might be able to pick up something at the other end."

"You're frigging daft, mate."

He gave her a broad grin. "That's what makes it all the more fun."

"You'll need extra equipment. NVGs, torch, grenades. Shit like that, yeah?"

"The whole package," Knocker allowed.

"If this turns to shit, don't you bring any trouble back to us."

Knocker shrugged. "If this turns to shit, I won't be coming back."

––––––––––

"I can't believe this shit," Tracey growled as she followed Knocker into the target house. Everything was a luminescent green from their NVGs, but once they were inside, Knocker took out a small flashlight. As expected, the building was empty.

Jensen found the door to the basement and went down. Once there, he walked around, looking for anything that might indicate there was a tunnel.

He'd seen lots of hiding places for them over the years: behind cupboards, wall rugs, under tables, a chicken pen, and even one hidden under a latrine.

It took Knocker only a few minutes to find this one. In the corner of the basement was a solid wood cupboard. Behind it was what Knocker was looking for. He slid it back, and the ragged opening of a tunnel appeared. He looked at Tracey. "Bingo."

They were both armed with suppressed M4 Carbines. Knocker turned off his flashlight, pulled down his NVGs, and switched on the infrared laser sights on his weapon. "Let's go and have a look."

They followed the tunnel for a good two hundred meters. At the end of that distance, it stopped, a wooden object of some description blocking further progress and covering their exit. "I'll bet my left nut that this is another bloody cupboard," he said in a harsh whisper.

"It has to be a basement in another building," Tracey surmised.

"Yeah, and it's probably loaded with flaming Jihadis looking for a nice piece of ass coming out of their cellar."

Knocker let the M4 hang by its strap as he tested the obstruction. It gave with pressure, and he slid it away from the opening as quietly as he could to reveal, as predicted, the darkened basement of another building. They walked through the opening and swept the room.

"What now?" Tracey asked.

"We have a look around."

"Shit, Knocker," she growled. "There could be a fucking shitload of terrorists up there, just waiting for some British wanker to come strolling up the stairs to say hello."

"Great, isn't it?"

He led the way up the stairs to a door. A light shone beneath the thin gap between the door and the floor. Knocker took his NVGs off and tried the handle. It turned, and the door latch came clear with an audible snick.

The former SAS operator eased his way through the opening, the M4 held at waist level in his right hand. The door led them into a short hallway, which was empty. Knocker seemed to mentally toss a coin as to which way to go.

A loud screech helped him make up his mind. The previously empty hallway now contained a man holding an AK-47. He had just brought it up to fire when Knocker double-tapped him in the chest. However, it wasn't enough. The man's trigger finger drew all the way back, and the AK rattled to life. Bullets stitched the ceiling as he fell, showering the hallway with debris. Not waiting, Knocker moved toward him. Tracey stayed behind him, covering his back.

"So much for quiet infiltration," she hissed.

"Shit happens," Knocker said as he shot the downed man again and stepped over his body.

The hallway opened into a large room, and Knocker swept it as he went. A door to his right was flung open and another armed man appeared. The former SAS man shot him before he could even get his weapon up. These guys had no idea and were totally unprepared, whereas Knocker was well-practiced at clearing rooms.

"Find us a way out of here," Knocker said as he covered the open door. Behind him, Tracey walked to his right and checked a second door.

She opened it and called, "This way."

Knocker followed her through and found himself in a darkened courtyard. Immediately, they dropped their NVGs over their eyes. Behind them, shouts could be heard from other rooms in what looked to be a larger compound.

"Someone made a cock-up," Knocker said.

"Do you think?" Tracey growled. "We need to get the hell out of here before we wind up dead."

Knocker pointed at a gate in the sandstone wall. "That way."

Tracey rushed toward it while Knocker covered the doorway. "Stuff it," he growled and took out a grenade. He pulled the pin and tossed it through the opening.

The thing exploded violently, blowing dirt and debris in every direction. He heard cries of pain and gave a satisfied nod.

"What the hell was that?" Tracey called.

"Just saying goodbye."

The gate led to a dimly lit street. Tracey said, "Which way, Captain Cook?"

"You know the natives killed him, right?"

"Uh-huh."

An automatic weapon opened fire from the darkness of a concealed alley down the street. Bullets whipped overhead, and the M4 in Knocker's hands came around. He squeezed the trigger. A long burst hammered out, and the shooter stopped firing as he took cover. "Back that way," the former

SAS man called to Tracey.

With her weapon up to her shoulder, she moved swiftly in the opposite direction while Knocker covered their rear.

"In here," she called quietly over her shoulder and slipped into an alley. Knocker followed her into the darkness. "That was fun," he said.

"Just keep moving and follow me," Tracey scolded. "I think I know how to get back to the vehicle."

"Lead the way."

"And shut up. I'm not talking to you."

Worldwide Drug Initiative HQ, El Paso, Texas

"All right, gather around," Thurston ordered her people as they entered the briefing room. "Find a seat and listen up."

Kane sat on a blue sofa next to Cara and Axe sat on her other side. Brick chose a stool off to one side. He had been distant ever since their return from Hawaii. The others took up various locations around the room and waited for their commander to start.

"Okay. The DEA came back to us earlier this afternoon with some information they gleaned from our resident Yakuza boss. He's given up his supplier in Brazil."

"What about the woman?" Kane asked.

"He doesn't know who she is, and Slick is no closer to finding her than he was a week ago. So, we concentrate on what we do know."

"Which is?"

"We're going to Brazil," Thurston said.

"Rio, baby," Axe said with a hint of excitement.

"Amapá, actually."

"Shit," growled Axe. "I hate fucking jungles."

"Why did you become a Recon Marine, then?" Cara asked him.

"I was told it paid good," he replied.

"Really?"

"True story."

"Who told you that crap?" Cara asked.

Axe looked at Kane.

The Team Reaper leader shrugged. "So, I lied." He paused. "Will we have Knocker back by the time we go operational?"

"No."

"Then I propose a stand-in," Kane put forward.

"Shit," muttered Traynor. "Don't pick me. I hate jungles just as much as Axe does."

Pete Traynor was a former DEA agent who did a lot of undercover work, hence the beard and tattoos that covered his arms. He was tall and broad-shoul-dered, and his hair matched his beard.

"I was thinking of Troy, ma'am."

"You want me to pull him off what I've got him

working on to come play with you and the others, Reaper?" Thurston asked.

"I'm sure your Special Projects team can do without him for a couple of days."

"I'll see what I can do."

"Yes, ma'am. Thank you."

"All right, let's talk about what we have."

Ferrero stepped forward. A large screen lit up, and the briefing began. The former DEA man pointed at the screen, which displayed a picture of a man who was distinctively Latino in looks, with a bushy mustache and wavy dark hair. In his right hand, he held a gold semi-automatic handgun.

"This, ladies and gents, is Alfredo Costa, known throughout Brazil as 'A Arma Dourada' or the Golden Gun."

"Where do they get these crazy names from?" Axe grumbled.

Ferrero continued. "He's one of the biggest cocaine manufacturers and distributors in Brazil. He resides in Rio, but most of his production is done in Amapá State. That keeps him at arm's length and makes him harder to prosecute."

"How much is he worth?" Traynor asked.

"Estimates say he's worth somewhere in the vicinity of two hundred billion, give or take."

"If we find any of it, can we keep it?" Axe asked.

Thurston fixed her gaze on the big man. "Sure. Maybe you can use some of it to pay for your accommodations at Leavenworth."

Axe smiled. "Glad you cleared that up, ma'am."

Ferrero said, "The mission will be twofold, to stop production and take Costa off the grid."

"How off the grid are we talking about?" Cara asked.

"He's to be taken alive. How it's done is up to the team."

"Where will you be setting up HQ?" Kane asked.

"We'll set up in Rio with the *Batalhão de Operações Policiais Especiais*," Ferrero explained.

"Who?" Reynolds asked.

"BOPE."

The *Batalhão de Operações Policiais Especiais,* or BOPE, was a Brazilian tactical police unit from the military police based in Rio. They performed a vast array of roles, from suppressing prison riots and breaking barricades set up by drug cartels to armed patrols and recon in remote terrain. By all accounts, they were good but brutal at their work. They had been referred to on multiple occasions as a death squad, and given that their badge bore a skull with a knife through it, one could understand why.

"I've heard they're good," Cara said, nodding her head.

"Killers in uniform," Kane announced. "I've seen them in action. You too, Luis. So why are we climbing into bed with them?"

"It was the only way to get in the country with

the blessing of the government," Ferrero explained.

"If these guys are so tough, why don't they send them after Cowboy Alf?" Axe asked.

Cara groaned. "You did not just say that."

"Say what?"

"'Cowboy Alf.'"

"You don't like it?" Axe wore a hurt expression on his face.

"Your worst yet."

"I could have called him 'Freddo Frog'."

"Good grief."

"To answer your question, Axe," Ferrero cut in, "Costa is popular among the people. While the government goes after his product and isn't afraid to engage his men, they hold back on going after the head of the snake. Their fear is if they do, they would have numerous riots on their hands."

"But it's all right for us to do it," Kane said, shaking his head.

"That's right."

"Hang on a minute," Brick said, speaking for the first time. "It sounds to me like if we go after Costa, we'll be doing it on our own. Am I right?"

"Yes, almost."

That changed things.

Kane said, "This guy has an army. What if we get jacked up and are neck-deep in the shit?"

"You'll have backup."

"Who?"

"A unit of BOPE shooters."

"I thought they didn't want to get involved?"

"Put it this way: once they cross that line, there's no going back. They're all volunteers who know the consequences should they get found out."

"Air cover?"

"Yes."

"And the government is all right with it?"

"The ones that count. We'll not leave you out on a limb. We'll have a Gray Eagle airborne at all times while you are operational."

"How do we insert?" Kane asked.

"That's up to you. I'll get Slick to give you all the intel he can get his hands on. Right, Slick?"

"You got it, Boss," Swift replied.

"Full package on the Gray Eagle, Brooke?"

"I'll see it has a couple of Hellfires and GBU-44s," Reynolds assured him.

Kane nodded. "The laser-guided bombs will be good. When do we go?"

"Two days."

"Sounds good to me. Does anyone have any further questions about the mission?"

When the room remained silent, they wrapped up. Kane and Cara grabbed Swift and informed him of what they wanted for the mission. That done, they headed to the armory to check equipment and ammo.

"I say we stick to the Four-Sixteens, and I'll take

a Four-Seventeen. Frag and smoke grenades. Maybe add the SAW and a couple of grenade launchers."

"We'll need to carry extra ammo," Kane said in agreement. "Once we get a plan worked out, we'll have a better idea of what other equipment we'll need."

Cara nodded. "Tell me about Troy."

Kane shrugged. "Not much to tell. We grew up together. School, Marines, Iraq. When I joined Recon, we went our separate ways."

"There must be something more than that. You got him a job here, and you want him on the team for this op."

"Believe me when I say I'd rather have Knocker on this one," Kane said. "But if I can't have him, I know Troy will be able to step up."

"All right, as long as you're positive," Cara said, not quite sure she believed him.

"He'll be fine."

CHAPTER 7

Mosul, Iraq.

Knocker was meeting with an MI6 informant when he realized he was in trouble. The problem was, he couldn't work out why he was being tracked by Westerners, not Middle Easterners. So far, he'd picked out three of them, all male. He was sure they were armed, even though it wasn't obvious. He reached down and felt for the reassuring butt of his Glock. All he had to do now was get out of there.

He reached for his cell and tried the number Tracey had given him, but there was nothing. The signal was being jammed. "Bollocks."

Knocker had two choices. His options were to stay here in a public place or find an alley and take his chances. As he looked around, assessing the odds, he saw another man. That made four. These guys were going nowhere. "All right, you tossers, let's see how good you really are."

Knocker rose from where he was seated and began heading toward an alley. Beside it stood one of the four who'd been watching him. He figured the man would do nothing until they were out of sight.

As he walked past him, Knocker glared into his face, letting him know he was aware of their presence. He said, "Rethink it, Wanker."

To his surprise, the man replied, "You're knackered, mate. Give it up."

Interesting, Knocker thought. British. This was worse than he thought. No sooner had the man behind him entered the alley than the former SAS man turned and drew his Glock. The stalker froze, having expected Knocker to run.

"Right, you sodding scouser, what gives?"

"Just take it easy—"

"Easy, *bullshit*. I'm going to fucking shoot you in five seconds if you don't tell me what is going on."

"Stand down, Jensen. You don't have a chance."

The woman's voice came from behind him. He frowned, but after as the words sank in, he said, "I don't fucking believe it."

He turned around and stood face to face with Ellen Grayson, alias Nemesis and a one-time member of the Cabal. "Where the hell did you come from?"

She'd changed. A wide-brimmed hat topped her long, almost cherry-red hair and sunglasses, and jeans and a cotton shirt covered her somewhat slimmer figure. "Drop the weapon, Knocker. There's no way out for you."

He glanced at the men flanking her and became aware that the number behind him had grown by another two. He looked at the weapon in his hand and passed it over with a nod of understanding. Miller took the weapon and tucked it into his pants. As he did so, Knocker looked skyward as though gazing at the sun.

"We've got a person willing to pay ten million to have you delivered to them alive, Knocker. You must have pissed him off something awful."

The former SAS man looked at Grayson and smiled. "Maybe I pissed in his porridge."

"Maybe. God knows you pissed in enough bowls over the years."

"Ten million, huh?"

She nodded. "Yes."

"It couldn't wait until I finish this op, could it?"

She gave him a regretful smile. "Not really. You still working for those pricks in El Paso?"

Knocker cocked his head to one side. "That was a good stunt you pulled back home, faking your death and all."

"I saw you there," she replied. "But that's quite enough for the time being. Come with us. We'll have ample time to talk."

———

The procession headed out the far end of the narrow alley, navigating several more streets and alleys to where two white 4X4s had been left out of the way. Knocker was placed in the back of the first with Grayson.

"So, what are you doing in Mosul?" Grayson asked him casually as though they were old friends catching up after a long time.

"Working," Knocker replied.

"Come on, Knocker, you can do better than that."

"All right. I'm chasing a ghost."

"Really?"

"I shit you not," he told her. "CIA got word he was here and asked for my help."

"Remember the last time you were here on an op?"

"Frigging balls-up, that was."

"Yeah, well…"

"So, what are you now, some kind of hunter or something?" Knocker asked her, curious as to why she would be involved.

Grayson gave a half-smile. "I offer a service to people who require it."

"What, now that your old business is screwed?"

"We're only lacking money," she told him. "Once we get on our feet again, the Cabal will be back."

"You're seriously not going to continue on with that shit, are you?" he asked in disbelief.

"The world is a bad place at the moment, Knocker. It needs people like us to straighten it out. Russia is doing what it wants, oppressing its people. China is expanding, taking away peoples' freedoms in Hong Kong. North Korea is still a threat, and the Middle East is heating up again. We're needed."

"So, are you the new Ares?"

"No, that was a pussy name. The new head of the Cabal is called Nemesis."

Knocker chuckled. "You really need to get a new press secretary. Shoot the fucker you've got now. He's bloody useless."

She looked offended and bit a retort back sharply. "You will never understand the power we have."

"What a load of bollocks. You're just a bunch of skiving tossers who sit around and measure how long their cocks are to see who has the biggest." He paused and stared before saying, "I'm not so certain you'd lose."

"Still got a sharp tongue, I see."

"Only for people who piss me off. We screwed you lot over twice already. Once more isn't going to take much."

"You, my dear chap, won't be around to see it."

"Don't be so sure," Knocker growled.

He turned away from her and looked out the window of the 4x4. Outside, the damaged city of Mosul flicked past. The situation made him angry. He wasn't done, not by a bloody longshot.

On the outskirts of Mosul, there was an old air-field used by the Iraqis, and before them, the Americans. The runway was long enough to accommodate many of the world's large aircraft, including a C-17. However, the one sitting on the runway now was a C-130. The two vehicles pulled up on the cracked tarmac and everyone climbed out, pushing Knocker before them as they walked up the ramp. Grayson indicated a seat on the left side near one of the small porthole-style windows for Knocker to sit in. A couple of minutes later, the rear ramp began to rise, and the interior of the plane darkened. The mighty engines spun up with a whine, and before long, all four were roaring.

Then the pilot released the plane's brakes, and it started moving. Knocker turned his head and looked out the window behind him, contemplating who the stupid asshole that was dumb enough to pay ten million for him was.

———————

Langley, Virginia

"This is bullshit," Joseph said as he looked at the pile of papers on his desk. He pressed the button on his desk phone and waited.

"Sir?" came a woman's voice from the other end.

"Barbara, find me some damned C4 so I can blow

something up."

"Paperwork, sir?"

"Is there any other kind in this place?"

"Would you like me to have a look at it for you?"

He sighed, "No, Barbara, it'll be fine."

"Just let me know if I can be of any assistance, sir."

"I will, thank you."

"By the way, Jim Hooker is here to see you."

Thank God. "Send him in. Please."

The door opened, admitting a tall, thin man. Once he'd closed the door, he turned and saluted.

"Cut that shit out," Joseph growled. "And sit down." He indicated the visitor chair across from him.

"Thank you, Admiral."

"What is it, Jim?"

Jim Hooker was a ten-year veteran of the United States Naval Intelligence community, but most recently, he had been promoted to head of the CIA Special Activities Division by Joseph. Therefore, at that point in time, the forty-year-old from Massachusetts was overseeing the operation in Mosul. He sighed. "Jensen has disappeared."

"Shit. Tell me what happened."

"We're not sure. He went out to run some surveillance and never came back to the MI6 safe house."

"What are we doing about it?"

"I'm putting extra resources on it, but I thought you should know."

"How long has he been gone?"

"Twenty-four hours."

"Do we have any idea what's happened to him?" Joseph asked.

"No. Best guess is that some branch of ISIS picked him up."

The admiral nodded. "Keep me updated, Jim."

"Yes, sir."

Worldwide Drug Initiative HQ, El Paso, Texas

"Thurston."

"Mary, it's Alex Joseph," the voice on the other end of the phone said.

"Yes, sir?"

"Knocker is missing in Mosul, Iraq."

The general remained silent as she processed what she'd just been told. After a long pause, Joseph said, "Mary, are you still there?"

"Yes, sorry, sir. What do you need from me?"

"Nothing, Mary. I've got my people on it. Besides, I know you're about to deploy on a mission of your own. This was just a courtesy call to give you a heads up."

"Thank you, sir. Does the general know?"

"I'll call him directly. My first thought was for you and the team."

"Yes, sir."

"I'll keep you advised, Mary."

The call disconnected, and Thurston cursed under her breath. She hit a button on the phone and waited. "Get Kane in here. Cara too."

A few minutes later, the Team Reaper commander and his second in command stood before her. They both knew something was wrong immediately. "What's up, ma'am?"

"Knocker is missing."

"Where?"

"Mosul."

"What was he doing in Mosul, ma'am?" Cara asked.

Thurston thought of playing the need-to-know card, but they were beyond that. "The CIA had a lead on The Ghost. Their informant there had gone off the grid, and they needed someone to find out what was happening. Now Knocker is gone, too."

"When do we leave?" Kane asked.

"Our mission remains the same, Reaper," Thurston told him. "The admiral is taking care of the other. He—"

"But, ma'am," Cara interrupted, "he's one of our own. We—"

"We need to stay focused on our current mission," the general growled. "We're wheels-up in a few hours. Has Troy arrived yet?"

"No, ma'am," Kane replied tautly.

"When he does, get him up to speed."

"Yes, ma'am."

"All right, that's all."

Cara left the general's office, but Kane remained. Thurston sighed. "All right, Reaper. Get it off your chest."

"We can't leave him out there, ma'am. You and I both know it."

"What do you propose I do about it?" she said, sitting back in her chair to look at him.

"You could send me to look for him," Kane replied. "Cara is quite capable of leading the team on a mission like this."

"That would leave the team one short, Reaper," Thurston pointed out. "That was why you asked for Troy."

"Send Pete in my place."

She shook her head. "No. This mission comes first. If we've heard nothing by the time we're done, I'll consider redeploying the team to Iraq."

"But that could take a week, ma'am. If not longer."

"I'm sorry, Reaper, but that's my decision." She stood, her countenance conveying that she would brook no further argument on the matter.

"Yes, ma'am."

———

"Hey, Reaper. What gives?"

Kane turned and saw a broad-shouldered man about his age and slightly taller grinning at him.

Reaper stepped forward with his hand out. "Good to see you, Troy."

Troy Barker's smile broadened. "Good to see you too, buddy. They tell me I got pulled because of you."

"Yes. I'm a man down, and I need a shooter. You up for it?"

"I think I can manage it. What are we doing?"

"I'll fill you in after I introduce you to the team. We're leaving in thirty minutes. I'll have Cara fix you up with some weapons. Follow me."

The rest of the team was in the briefing room, waiting to roll out. As Kane and Troy entered, every head turned to take in the newcomer before he was introduced. Axe looked at Troy and asked, "Does this one speak American?"

Troy frowned and looked at Kane. "Don't ask," he said with a shake of his head. "You don't want to know."

"The last guy Reaper hooked us up with had trouble speaking American," Axe elaborated. "Hell, he had trouble speaking at all."

"Where is he?" Troy asked.

Everyone averted their eyes except for Kane. "He's MIA. Mosul."

"Shit. Sorry."

"We all feel like we're going the wrong way, but it's not our call."

Troy was about to speak when Ferrero entered the room. "All right, get your gear. We're leaving."

CHAPTER 8

Khartoum, Sudan

The meeting place was not the same as the last one, and they were met by a different man. Grayson sat at a small table outside a Khartoum café, drinking something that was supposed to pass for coffee. It tasted like what you would get if a donkey shit in a pot and you boiled it for thirty minutes.

Opposite her sat Knocker, his bound hands under the table while they waited for the pickup. Two tables away sat Miller, Collins, and Royston, their handguns out of sight on their laps. The three bodyguards and their boss were wired with comms so they could hear everything that was said. Grayson wore her usual wide-brimmed hat and sunglasses to hide her identity from prying eyes above. She looked down at her watch. "We give them five more minutes, then we're gone. I don't want to sit out here in the open any longer than necessary."

"Getting nervous, Ellen?" Knocker asked with a smile.

"Shut up, Jensen."

Knocker looked at the street. There were pedestrians everywhere, but one caught the former SAS man's eye. He was tall with a dark beard and stood sequestered in a doorway, holding a cell phone. He had to be one of the bad guys. Knocker guessed that if he'd seen him, so had the security team.

Moments later, two 4X4s came toward them. Grayson straightened and said, "Heads up."

Her team readied themselves in case something like a double-cross went down. Out of sight was the second team—her backup.

The vehicles stopped on the side of the street, and six men climbed out. All except one were armed with AK-47s. The remaining man had no weapon and wore a suit. Knocker frowned. The bastard in the suit was definitely Arab. However, the others wore bulging thawbs and face coverings.

The bulges were unmistakably vests. He looked at their hands, and he could tell right away that these guys were not Arab. They were Caucasian, possibly trained shooters gone over to the dark side. The man in the suit said, "The master will be happy to see that you have accomplished what he asked."

"How about we talk about money?" Grayson said curtly, cutting to the chase, not willing to remain there any longer than necessary.

"Yes, of course."

"Who are you, anyway?"

"I am no one."

"What about your friends?" Knocker asked. "Where are they from? Russia? Bosnia? Britain?"

One of the men moved nervously. Knocker glanced at Grayson. "Fucking hopeless, aren't they?"

"Still got it, huh?" she commented.

"They're amateurs."

One of the men stepped forward and made to clip the former SAS man with the butt of his weapon. Knocker expected it and moved swiftly. Even though his wrists were bound, he deflected the blow and had the attacker on the ground in a couple of heartbeats.

Before he knew it, weapons were pointed at him, ready to fire. Knocker looked at the shooters. "You cocks are having a laugh, aren't you? You won't kill me. Your boss would do the same to you."

"Put the guns down," Grayson told them. "Before someone gets hurt."

The men lowered their weapons, and Knocker straightened. He sensed the movement behind him but had no time to turn and meet the threat. Lights flashed and he dropped to his knees, his ears ringing. Knocker shook his head to try to rid it of the fuzzy feeling, but his attacker wasn't done with him yet. Another swipe and he fell forward, unconscious.

Grayson winced. "Was that really necessary?"

The man who'd struck Knocker glared at her from behind the face-covering before signaling to another of the shooters to give him a hand. As they dragged Knocker away, the man in the suit said, "Shall we conclude our business?"

"What's going to happen to him?" she asked, a little annoyed by the situation.

"What do you care?"

The man's insolence rubbed Grayson the wrong way, and she thought that had things been a little clearer, she'd have shot him in the face. "I was curious."

"Don't be."

Grayson opened the laptop in front of her and hit a couple of keys. She then turned it and pushed it toward the man. "All you need to do is put your account number in."

The man smiled mirthlessly, took a small electronic device from his pocket, and plugged it in. "Just in case."

Two minutes later, the transaction was done.

The man bowed. "Thank you for your service. I'm sure our master will reach out again should he have further need of you."

"I'm sure he will."

The man returned to the vehicle he'd arrived in. The shooters did the same. Once they were gone, Grayson was about to call her perimeter in when Flint's voice came over the comms. "We've got movement, ma'am. I'm thinking ten to twenty shooters. Looks like our friend wants to end our business arrangement permanently."

She looked down the street, which was suddenly eerily deserted. "Where are they, Mister Flint?" Grayson's voice was calm, controlled.

"They're everywhere."

"All right, fall back to the vehicles. Quickly."

No sooner had the words passed her lips than the first burst of gunfire echoed down the street. "Everyone move," Grayson snapped, drawing her hidden SIG Sauer P226. Her bodyguards formed a defensive ring around her, and they moved down the street toward the SUVs. A shooter appeared in front of them, and Miller fired twice. The man fell to the dirty street, his weapon spilling from his grip. Beside Miller, Collins fired his weapon, and another shooter died.

By then, they had reached the SUVs, and Grayson climbed into the back.

More killers appeared as the three bodyguards followed their boss into the vehicle. Rounds ricocheted harmlessly off the armored exterior. Flint and the operations team reached them, all of them firing their M6 carbines at unseen threats. Once they'd climbed into the lead vehicle, Grayson's comms lit up. "There's a lot of the bastards, ma'am. What do you want to do? They're setting up roadblocks to the east and west of us. I don't think we're supposed to leave."

Grayson asked, "Are you still on-station?"

For a moment one might have thought she was talking to Flint, but another voice came back through her earpiece. "Yes, ma'am."

"Light the fuckers up."

"On the way."

Overhead, watching their every move, was an armed Chinese-made CH-4 Rainbow UAV. Under the wings, attached to six hardpoints, were air-to-ground missiles that were about to be unleashed upon the attackers below. Grayson said, "Hit a roadblock before you expend all your ordnance, understood?"

"Roger that."

The first explosion rocked the vehicles they sat in; it was that close. A pall of dust rose down the street, evidence of the missile strike. Another rocked the immediate surroundings and Grayson said, "Get us out of here, Mister Miller."

The two SUVs shot forward, bullets striking their exterior. In the rear seat, the woman known as Nemesis watched as another missile came in and exploded violently to the north of them. A voice said, "Roadblock north of you is clear, ma'am."

"Thank you. Is there any sign of the two vehicles that left the rendezvous point?"

"They are traveling south, ma'am. They were joined by another two."

"Follow them for as long as you can. I want to know where they go."

Miller turned in his seat and asked, "Where

to, boss?"

"Back to the plane. I want to be in the air inside the hour."

"Are we going after him?"

"I can think of fifty million reasons why we should, can't you?"

———————

Nemesis and her team were in the air when her ISR team reached out. "When we had to call time, ma'am, they were still headed south. My guess would be either South Sudan or Eritrea. I would rule out Ethiopia."

"Why?"

"I don't think that is an option."

"If you had to go with your best guess, what would it be?"

"South Sudan."

"All right, let's get some people in there and see what we can find out."

"Right away. You might want to check your encrypted emails, ma'am. Another job has just come through."

Grayson grabbed her laptop and opened it. She punched in a code, then a second to access her emails. There was one new message. Opening it, she read it twice and once finished, reached beside her for a set of headphones and put them on. Into the bar mic, she said, "Flint, I want to see you."

A minute or so later, he sat beside her. "What is it?"

"Another job."

"Where are we headed?"

"Europe."

"Do we know the client?"

"Gustaw Marek."

"*The* Gustaw Marek? The Polish Defense Minister who disappeared a while back after his drug empire was brought down by—"

"Yes, the very one." She cut him off, needing to hear no more.

"Are we going to meet him?" Flint asked.

"Miller and I will. I may take one more with us. You take the rest of the team back to the island. Find out where that asshole went so I can collect on his head."

"Yes, ma'am."

Samokov, Macedonia

The village of Samokov is nestled in a small but lush valley with large hills on either side. The village itself is long and narrow and is situated in the municipality of Makedonski Brod, North Macedonia.

It was here that Grayson and her two-man escort found Gustaw Marek, who now lived in exile in a very large and lavish white house with a team of twelve mercenaries hired from various European countries that made up his personal bodyguard.

Time had not treated him well. The former Polish minister's graying hair was now white, his shoulders rounded with the weight of grief he still felt from the death of his son. Added to that was bitterness, a deep-rooted hatred for the ones responsible for everything he'd lost. It was time to make them pay.

"I want them all dead," he growled, his eyes sparkling with anger. By "them", he meant Team Reaper and everyone else at the Worldwide Drug Initiative.

"That is a tough ask, Mister Marek," Grayson said.

His eyes narrowed. "I have money."

"How much, Mister Marek? Something like this will not come cheap. I've experienced firsthand what they are capable of."

Marek climbed out of his leather lounge and walked to a large bulletproof window that afforded him a view of the valley and its greenery. "How does fifty million sound?"

Grayson took a deep breath. That much money in the Cabal's coffers would go a long way toward putting it back together again. To do that, she needed money, lots of it. Besides, it was no fun being a one-person Cabal. The more money she had, the more people were likely to come out of the shadows and join her. "Do you have that much, Mister Marek?"

"I have three times that much. Do you want the

job or not?"

"I'll take it. However, I want half the money up front. If you're not willing to pay that, we can't do business."

"Twenty-five million seems an awfully steep upfront payment. What if you fail?"

"Then you and I are each out twenty-five million dollars."

"I guess it's a risk I'm going to have to take."

"Good. You'll hear from me when the job is done. One way or the other."

Marek's face turned into a mask of hatred. "Make sure they know who is responsible, do you hear? Make sure they know!"

———

Somewhere in South Sudan

Knocker's head still hurt where the bastards had put him to sleep. He made a mental note to find out which one was responsible and feed him his bollocks. The heat inside wherever they were keeping him was almost unbearable. His hands were still tied, and the hood they had put over his head was still in place. The one thing he did know about his captors was that they all spoke good old UK English.

Knocker figured he was locked in a tin shed. The heat and the noises filtering through from outside told him that, plus the sound the door had made when they'd locked him in. He'd asked them a number of questions, but no one had answered. They'd then left him to wait.

He tried his bonds again but got nowhere. They were starting to go numb from the pressure of the plastic flexicuffs.

The door opened, scraping the ground as it was pulled back. Two men entered and dragged the former SAS man to his feet. "Hey, you guys want to get rid of these flexicuffs?"

They shoved him forward, and he staggered into the corrugated iron wall. Knocker grunted. "I guess that means no."

The hands grabbed him again, this time guiding him through the opening and out into the hot African sun.

"Where are we going?" he asked and received another forceful push from behind. He staggered and went to his knees, only to be dragged up and shoved roughly forward again.

"You know, if you keep pushing me around, it's going to take us forever to get wherever it is we're going, right?"

"Shut the fuck up," one of the men snapped.

"I would," Knocker said, "but it's hard to have a conversation that way."

One of the men hit him in the kidneys, which elicited a grunt of pain. From between clenched teeth, the former SAS man snarled, "Fucking sissy."

The ground beneath Knocker's boots felt hard-packed, so he figured he was being guided across some kind of parade square. He heard someone speaking from a distance and frowned as he tried to make out the language. Then it came to him; it was Lokoya. They'd taken him to South Sudan.

The men escorted him to a hut built from sticks, mud, and grass. It had once been a small village but had been taken over by the terrorists who had moved the resident villagers out. Now it was a training camp for The Ghost's men.

Once Knocker was inside the hut, they removed his hood and forced him to sit on the hard-packed earth floor.

Knocker looked around the dark interior until he picked out the lone figure seated near the far wall. The figure—a man—looked up. Knocker blinked and cocked his head to one side. "You? You're the fool who paid ten million for me? You're The Ghost?"

"Welcome to South Sudan," said Lieutenant Dan Best with a smile.

Knocker couldn't believe what he was seeing. "You're still alive. I can't believe it."

"No thanks to you," Best said, the bitterness in his voice more than evident.

"I don't know what to say."

"What could you say? You left me to the mercy of the Islamic Caliphate."

"They obviously didn't kill you."

Best grunted. "They made me the man I am today."

"A murdering wanker?"

"I have you to thank for that. For everything I went through."

"Well, say thanks, and I'll be on my way," Knocker told him.

"I'll thank you all right, Jensen," the terrorist growled. "I'll thank you in front of the world."

Knocker gritted his teeth. "Just cut my fucking head off and get it over and done with."

Best struggled to his feet with the aid of a crutch and reached for a four-legged walking frame the former SAS man hadn't noticed. It was then Knocker remembered that on their last meeting in Mosul, the Brit's Achilles tendons had been severed on both legs. That was what had prompted Best to ask him to kill him. Knocker hadn't been able to bring himself to do it and had left him behind, still breathing.

Best struggled toward him and stopped a few feet short of the former SAS operator. "You're not going to die fast, Jensen. Just like you wouldn't kill me fast when I begged you to. Instead, you left me behind. But have no fear. By the time I'm finished with you, you'll beg for death, just like I did."

"You're bloody insane."

"No, I've seen the light. Left behind by my own people, I did what I had to do to survive. And found the only person to help me through the worst of it and out the other side."

"Who? Your mother?" Knocker sneered. He'd rather die quickly than linger, hoping for rescue.

Best looked over Knocker's head and nodded. There was movement behind him, and he turned his head as a woman walked past him. She was thin, of average height, and wore pants and a tank top. A thin stiletto in a gold sheath rested on her right thigh.

"This is Khazbika," Best explained. "She's from Chechnya. She is the best thing that ever happened to me. She nursed me back to health and gave me the strength I needed to go on."

"What does she do? Suck cock?" Knocker was willing to try anything at that moment. The last thing he wanted was to be heinously tortured over the coming days.

Best smiled. "I see what you are doing, but it will not get you the quick death you desire."

The terrorist nodded at the woman.

Khazbika stepped around behind Knocker and drew her stiletto. Before he could move, she plunged the razor-sharp blade into the top of his shoulder. It only entered about an inch and a half, grating on bone as it penetrated. The former SAS man cried out and his body stiffened. The knife withdrew and

Knocker gasped for breath, heavy beads of sweat forming on his brow. "Fucking bitch. How about you wrap that pretty mouth of yours around my knob, and we'll see if you're any good at that?"

The knife went in again, almost in the same place. Khazbika leaned down and put her mouth close to his ear. "If you want me, you only have to say so."

She bit his ear as the knife came free of his flesh, and he gasped again. The sweat flowed freely now, his shirt wetter than it had been when he was locked in the shed.

Best smiled. "That will do, my dear."

Khazbika stepped back and put the knife away, but not before she wiped it on Knocker's shirt. Best said, "Now we will leave you for a couple of days to let the wounds heal before we bring you back for more special treatment. Perhaps next time, we will pull out some of your fingernails. Nothing too bad. You see, I have no wish for you to die right away. I want it to last so I can enjoy your misery the way others enjoyed mine. Take him away."

The hood went back over Knocker's head, and he was returned to the tin shed where he would bathe in the heat and suffer the misery of his pain. And this was just the beginning.

CHAPTER 9

Amapá State, Brazil

Large water drops fell from the canopy of the rainforest. The torrential downpour had stopped about an hour before, leaving the team saturated to the skin. Axe walked point while Brick brought up the rear. The former's voice came through the comms. "I hate frigging jungles. Especially the equatorial bastards."

"Did you say something, sweetheart?" Cara asked him as she wiped her brow just below the soaked bandana wrapped around her head. "Do you need me to come up there and kiss it better for you?"

"Don't make promises you can't keep, ma'am."

"You're right; your new girlfriend might not like it. You got that new tattoo yet?"

Kane, walking second behind Axe, grinned to himself and waited for the comments to come. Axe had a habit of becoming too invested with his girls early on and was notorious for getting their names tattooed when he figured he was in love.

"You must be running out of room, Axe," Brick said. "You'll have to start getting them put on your ass soon."

"Very funny," he muttered into his comms.

"You don't have my name tattooed anywhere on your person, do you?" Cara asked.

"Why would I have your name tattooed on my Johnson, ma'am?"

"Now that is something I can't unsee," Cara said. She looked through the undergrowth and could see Kane's shoulders trembling as he held himself back to keep from bursting out laughing.

"She said 'person', you dick," Brick growled, "not Johnson."

"Oh."

"Reaper One? Zero. Sitrep, over."

Kane pressed the transmit button on his comms. "Zero, this is Reaper One. We're about five klicks from our target. ETA approximately twenty-one-hundred hours. Over."

"Good copy, Reaper One."

"What's the latest intel, Zero, over?"

"We're still gathering it, Reaper One. Latest estimate is fifteen, that's one-five, tangos on target."

"Roger that, Zero."

"We'll have confirmation once you arrive on-site, over."

"Copy, Zero. Reaper One out."

The team had parachuted into the jungle six hours before. It had been a daylight jump, which made it easier for them to hit their small LZ. That was why they had been dropped the extra distance from their target.

The plan was to reach the drug factory that night and set up an OP. They would occupy that position the following day and assault the next night. The factory was built on a wide river, and the plan called for two of them, Kane and Troy, to utilize the water to infiltrate the drug lab area and plant charges. Axe would set up the SAW while Cara provided overwatch. Brick would be on Cara's shoulder as a one-man QRF.

"Axe, hold up," Kane said into his comms. "Swap with Troy."

"I'm good, Reaper," Axe replied.

"Just do it. Everyone, take five."

After Axe swapped with Troy, Kane sought him out. The big former Recon Marine was seated on a large tree root, taking a drink from his canteen.

"What's going on, Axe?"

Axe looked up at Kane. "What do you mean?"

"You know exactly what I mean. Troy."

"How about you spell it out, Reaper?"

Kane nodded. "All right. You seem to have a problem with him being on the team."

"How can I when I don't know him?" Axe asked,

avoiding the question.

"And there it is. You don't know him, Axe, so give him a chance. He's a good operator. Why do you think Thurston put him into the new Special Projects venture?"

"Yeah, well. He's got to prove himself, hasn't he?"

"He's already proved himself to me. Just give him a chance."

"All right. I—"

"Danger close! Danger close!" the harsh whisper came through the comms. The voice was unmistakably Troy's.

"Everybody into the jungle," Kane said hurriedly.

The team took to the green stuff and blended in with their surroundings. Their weapons were suppressed, but they didn't want to use them unless there was no other choice. It was best to let whoever it was slide right past and go on their merry way. Missing people inspired others to ask questions.

Kane laid down on his stomach. His Heckler and Koch 416 was at his shoulder and ready to use. He blinked sweat from his eyes as he waited for the threat to appear.

Troy's voice came across the comms again, this time quieter and calmer. "Six tangos inbound. All armed."

"Are they militia, Reaper Three?" Kane had given his friend Knocker's call sign for the mission.

Troy's answer was to break squelch once.

Yes, Kane thought. *And for him to signal that way, they must be almost on top of him.*

Then came a number of voices followed by laughter. It sounded like they were joking about something, not a good thing to do when on patrol in the jungle. Then again, this was their backyard, and they weren't expecting Team Reaper to be in it.

The voices grew louder, and so did the passage of the militiamen. Branches cracked as they trod carelessly. Kane shook his head.

Then he saw them. At first it was their heads bobbing above the undergrowth, then the rest as they drew closer. The voices became clearer, and he could see their faces.

They were dressed in an assortment of pants and shirts containing more holes than a golf course. They all wore sweat-stained bandanas, and their faces were grimy and unshaven. They were all well-armed, each man carrying a Taurus T4 assault rifle with webbing that held extra ammunition. However, there was no body armor to be seen.

They walked past the hidden team, oblivious to their presence. The voices slowly ebbed with their passage and then they were gone, swallowed by the steaming jungle.

"Is that it, Reaper Three?" Kane whispered into his comms.

"Roger that. We're all clear up here."

"Good catch."

The team came out from their hiding places and gathered on the trail.

Kane said to Brick, "Go and check our backtrail. Once we start moving again, trail us by thirty meters. That way, we can make sure they don't surprise us coming the other way."

"Roger that."

The team continued moving until dark when they took another break. There were no signs of any other patrols.

Onward they went through the thick jungle. Even though the sun had gone away, the air was still humid and held the dense smell of damp vegetation.

"Reaper One, copy?"

It was Cara.

"Good copy, Reaper Two."

"We've reached Woodstock. I say again, we've reached Woodstock. How copy?"

"Good copy, Reaper Two. We've reached Woodstock."

_____

Amapá State, Brazil

It was an hour before dawn, and Kane was taking over the next watch from Cara. He found her in a position where she could use her scope to see the compound where the drug lab was set up. "How are we looking?"

"Just the roving patrols," Cara said. "Other than that, it's reasonably quiet. Once the sun comes up, we'll get a better picture."

"Get some rest. I'll wake you if anything happens. Once we know more later we can tweak our plan to suit."

"Roger that."

However, instead of going off to rest, Cara lay down beside Kane and closed her eyes. He looked at her and smiled. She'd been with him from the beginning. She and Axe were the only original team members left in the field. Carlos had done enough, and thinking of his family, he left the team. The other was Conrad Hawkins or Hawk, as he'd been known. Unfortunately, he'd been killed on a mission in Guatemala.

Sure, most of the others had been there since day one—Ferrero, Traynor, Reynolds, Teller, and Swift. Thurston had come along a bit later when the WDI needed streamlining, as had Brick, Knocker, and Rosanna Morales, their doctor. But over the many missions they had completed, they had grown into a tight-knit family and had each other's backs. But the bond between Kane and Cara was special.

After a few minutes, he heard her breathing change as she slipped into a deep sleep. He took her HK417 and did a sweep of the compound.

The night insects started to buzz around Kane's head, and he had to concentrate to block out their incessant whine. There was a rustle to his left in the undergrowth. Kane turned his head, and from her slumber, Cara said, "That'll be George."

"Who's George?" Kane asked.

"The jaguar."

"The what?"

"You know what a jaguar is, right?"

"Of course, I know what a jaguar is."

"Then you know George. He's fine."

"Let's hope he's not hungry."

"If he is, you're stuffed. He seems to like me."

"Great."

Cara went back to sleep while Kane waited for the sun to come up. When it finally rose, it brought with it the thick, cloying humidity that was all too familiar to him. By the time Cara came awake, his clothes were soaked with perspiration. She turned her head to him. "I'm beginning to see why Axe hates the jungle."

She sat up and reached into her pocket for a rag. Then she removed her body armor, followed by her top. Underneath, she wore no bra, just a tank top. She took that off and wet the rag before wiping herself down, trying to get rid of all the salt where everything rubbed. Kane asked, "You want a hand with that?"

She winked at him. "Somehow, I don't think so."

Once Cara was done, she put everything back on. "What's happening?"

"Not much. They haven't started to stir yet."

Cara rolled onto her belly and reached for her 417. Kane handed it over, and she did a sweep of the compound. The roving patrols were still out but were undoubtedly ready to change shifts. She said, "Are they still on a five-minute schedule?"

"Pretty much. They are keeping to that time while walking the perimeter."

She moved the scope and focused on the river, which snaked lazily past the rear of the compound. Her scope traveled slowly over the surface until she saw a swirl in the water. She stopped, and what appeared to be a rough log surfaced. Cara's lips pressed together. "You and Troy won't be going in by the river."

"Why?"

"A caiman just surfaced near the bank."

"That's screwed, then," Kane said. "Zero Two, copy?"

"Read you Lima Charlie, Reaper One," Carlos Arenas responded.

"Did you get a good sleep, buddy?"

"Like a baby, *amigo*. What can I do for you?"

"The infil point is screwed. We've got water lizards patrolling the shore."

"Copy."

"Do we still have a bird in the air?"

"Not for much longer."

"Copy," Kane replied, then he said, "Bravo Four, copy?"

"Copy, Reaper One," Swift replied.

"Our infil is compromised, so I need a new plan. I need some up-to-date pictures of the compound. Send them to the Toughbook when they're ready."

"Will do, standby."

Five minutes later, Swift came back on the air. "Reaper One, you should have all you need. Bravo Four out."

"Thanks, Bravo Four. Reaper One out."

There was movement in the undergrowth, and Brick appeared. "I see you're both still alive."

Kane nodded. "You all right to take over?"

"Bright as a button."

"Good. We're going back to rejig the plan. Our infil is compromised. I'll give you an update when I have one."

"Roger that."

———

"Nothing changes except the insertion points," Kane said. "Take down the perimeter rovers before we set the charges."

Cara nodded. "It's the only way."

Kane looked at the others. "We all get a vote."

Everyone agreed.

"All right, let's work it out in full." Kane stabbed a finger at the picture on the screen. "Troy and I will go in here. Brick and Axe come in from the south. We take out the perimeter guards, place the charges, and get out. The charges will be set to go off just before they change the guard after dawn. It will cause maximum confusion, so we can take them all down then."

"You want me to set up on overwatch like we worked out?"

"Yes. You'll be crucial if they start reorganizing."

"What if you're bumble-footed like Axe and it all goes to shit?" Brick asked with a grin.

"Then we continue the mission the hard way. But make sure you shoot Axe first."

Brick snorted. "Roger that."

"There you go again," said Axe. "Picking on innocents like me. And I'm not bumble-footed. I can get around this jungle a lot damned quieter than you."

"Except if you see a snake," Cara said.

"There's no harm in being afraid of snakes."

"I can't understand it. A big tough guy like you who runs into all kinds of dangerous situations is scared of a little ground-dwelling animal—"

"Reptile," Axe interrupted.

"What?"

"Reptile, ma'am. They're reptiles."

"Maybe we should go back to Australia," Kane said, enjoying seeing the big man squirm.

"Don't even go there, Reaper. You think jungles are bad? *Everything* kills you in that country. They have all the world's top deadliest snakes except a handful. Even that British guy won't go there."

Kane frowned. "What British guy?"

"That Steve Backshall guy."

"The dude from Deadly Sixty?" Troy asked, speaking up for the first time.

Axe's eyes widened. "That's him. He was told to go film one of his shows there and he refused."

"Why?"

"Because there are more than sixty deadly animals there, that's why."

Cara slapped her forehead. "You're a dick."

Axe looked at her innocently. "Why?"

She looked at the others. "Who is going to tell him?"

They all moved back with disinterested expressions on their faces. "Tell me what?" asked Axe.

Cara shook her head. "Don't leave it up to me. I'll just shoot him."

Kane gave her a resigned look. "It might be best."

"Great."

"I'll do it," Troy said. "Can't be a man down before we even start. Axe, come with me. I'm afraid I've got some bad news for you."

———

Kane eased through the undergrowth, pushing a frond away as quietly as possible. The surrounding jungle was green, made that way by the NVGs he was wearing. Through that illumination, the thin, rail-straight line from the laser sights reached out like a lance finding its next victim.

Behind Kane came Troy. The team leader was impressed with the way his friend had slipped back into the environment of going downrange.

They reached the perimeter of the compound and paused. Kane took a knee and pressed the transmit button on his comms. "Reaper Four, sitrep?"

"Reaper Four and Five in position."

"Reaper Two?"

"Reaper Two set."

"Move in."

Kane took one step forward, and all hell broke loose.

CHAPTER 10

Amapá State, Brazil

The explosion was loud and bright, so much so that every member of the team gasped and reacted by closing their eyes against the flare in the NVGs they wore. Kane blinked to clear his vision.

"What the fuck was that?" Axe growled into his ear through the comms.

"Keep the channel clear," Kane snapped. "Zero Two, did you get that?"

"Roger, Reaper. We saw it," Arenas replied.

"What—" His next words were cut off by gunfire ripping through the night.

He dove to the ground, and behind him, Troy did the same. Bullets tore through the undergrowth, cutting down foliage like a scythe as they went. "Reaper Two, can you see anything?"

"Reaper, I have a—" Another explosion.

"Say again, Reaper Two."

"Pull back, Reaper One. Pull back."

Knowing enough not to question her, he issued the command over the net. "All call signs withdraw. I say again, all call signs withdraw."

Each team member checked in as the night was lit up by whatever was happening. Explosions and gunfire continued to tear the darkness apart as they pulled back. Once back at their OP, Kane dropped beside Cara. "What's going on?"

"I'm not sure. There's a lot of confusion down there."

"Reaper One, this is Bravo, copy?"

"Read you Lima Charlie, General. Over."

"Reaper, from where we are, it looks like a large force is attacking the drug compound. They came in from the north."

"Do you have any idea who they are?"

"Not as of yet."

"We'll just sit tight and eat dirt until it's all over then, ma'am."

"That might be best."

"Reaper One, out."

For the next twenty-two minutes, the explosions and gunfire continued. Then it died to the occasional sporadic shot. After that, nothing, just an eerie silence as the jungle returned to its quiet self.

The sun started to rise in the east, and with it came the heat and the early morning birds. As the landscape brightened, Cara was able to get her first decent look at the mysterious interlopers.

"That's one for the books," she said in a low voice while she looked through the scope atop the 417.

"What is it?" Kane asked.

"If I had to hazard a guess, I'd say the force down there is French marines."

"From French Guiana?"

"That would be my guess, yes."

"What the hell are they doing here?"

"Same thing we are by the looks of it."

"Zero, copy?" Kane said.

"Copy, Reaper One."

"We think our new visitors are French marines from across the border."

"I'll have the general look into it, Reaper. What are—"

"Wait one, Zero."

As Kane looked down at the compound, Cara asked, "What are they doing?"

The marines had organized six prisoners in a line in an open area of the compound. One of the marines—they assumed he was an officer—stood apart from the rest. He said something and waved his hands as he did. Two marines broke away from the others and dragged a single prisoner forward.

"This isn't good, Reaper." There was concern in Cara's voice.

Without hesitation, the officer drew his sidearm

and shot the prisoner in the head.

"Shit," Kane hissed through clenched teeth. "Zero, they just shot a prisoner. Please advise."

"Wait one, Reaper."

"You'd better hurry up. They're about to shoot another one."

The two marines had returned to the line of prisoners and were dragging another one forward. They forced him to his knees in front of the officer, and the man shot him in the head as well.

"Damn it, Zero."

"Stand down, Reaper One." It was Thurston.

"Ma'am?"

"You heard me. Let it play out."

"Yes, ma'am."

A third prisoner was brought forward and placed at the feet of the sadistic officer. This time, however, the bound man wasn't shot in the head like his compatriots. He was shot in the leg.

"He's after information," Cara said.

"Maybe," Kane replied.

The sharp crack of the handgun reached out again as the prisoner was shot in the other leg. "This is horseshit," Kane growled.

The officer shot the prisoner a third time.

Kane put out his hand. "Give me your weapon, Reaper Two."

Cara turned her head to stare at Kane. "What are you going to do, Reaper?"

"I'm putting an end to this."

"Reaper—"

"Your weapon," he grated.

"If you shoot that officer, you'll bring all kinds of hell down on yourself."

"Give me the damn weapon."

Cara sighed and passed the 417 to him. Kane took it and tucked the butt into his shoulder. He looked through the sights until he was assured that he had a good bead on his target, then he squeezed the trigger.

The French marine officer's head snapped back, and he dropped like a stone. Kane pressed his transmit button and said, "Zero, Reaper Team has been compromised. We're pulling out."

"What the fuck was that?" Cara whispered vehemently.

"I don't have time for this, Cara," Kane replied.

"Well, make time, dammit."

They had covered only a couple of klicks since they'd left their OP, and Cara had stewed about what had happened all the way. Now she was ready to take the issue head-on with her commander and friend.

"I shot the prick, that's what it was. All right?"

"You were told not to. They'll cook your fucking

grits for that."

Kane went to turn away, but Cara wasn't done. She grabbed his shoulder and turned him forcefully. "Talk to me, damn it."

He stared into her eyes and saw that she wouldn't be deterred. "All right. I was in Africa on a mission once, years ago. We were in the Congo, actually. We came across a small village the local militia had taken over. They gathered the locals in one spot and started to shoot them. I radioed it in and was told to stand down. We sat there and watched every one of those villagers get murdered. It took four hours, and we did nothing so our presence wouldn't be compromised. I wasn't going to watch it happen again."

"Shit, Reaper, those assholes weren't villagers. We probably would have killed them anyway."

"They were prisoners, Cara. We don't shoot prisoners, no matter who they are."

"You getting soft?"

"Maybe."

"Well, you'd better harden the fuck up because when we get back, Thurston will chow down on that ass of yours, and it won't be pleasant."

"I fully expect it. Now, move out."

WDI Safehouse, Rio de Janeiro

"What happened?" Thurston snapped after pulling Ferrero aside so no one could hear her.

"I don't know. I told him to stand down."

"Yet, he didn't."

"So it would seem."

"As soon as he gets back, he's grounded," she said, making it sound like she was referring to a schoolboy.

"What do you mean?" Ferrero asked.

"I mean, he's off missions until I decide whether or not I'm going to kick his ass off the team."

"Surely you can't be serious, Mary?" Ferrero stated.

"Damn right, I'm serious. Find me another commander for the team who can stand in."

"What about Cara?"

"No, I want someone from outside. If you can't do it, then I frigging will. Do you understand me?"

"Yes, ma'am."

"Good. I want the recommendation by the end of the day, and the operator here tomorrow or the next day at the latest."

Ferrero stared at her for a moment before asking, "Any news on Knocker?"

"Not a damned word," she replied and stormed off.

The deputy commander of the WDI sensed someone behind him. He turned and saw Traynor standing there. "How much did you hear?"

"Most of it."

"Keep it to yourself, Pete."

"My lips are sealed. But I'm here for another reason."

"What is it?"

"It looks like the team has picked up a tail."

"How bad?"

"It's the French marines."

"That's all we need."

"Where are they?" Ferrero barked as he looked at the big screen in their operations room.

"Here," Swift said, tapping several keys on his board. The picture zoomed out and showed the heat signatures of the following force of French marines.

"How far behind the team are they?"

"Maybe a klick. They're moving fast. Faster than Kane and the others."

"They're on a mission, then. Looks like Reaper's lack of discipline pissed them off." He picked up a headset and put it on. "Reaper One, copy?"

"Go ahead, Zero."

"You've got tangos coming up fast on your six. Advise you put a little pep in your step, over."

"Any idea who they are, Zero?"

"Yes. The French marines."

"Roger. Please advise."

"Are you going to follow my damned orders this time, Reaper?"

There was a long pause. "Say again, Zero."

"Get the hell out of there, Reaper. Don't slow down."

"Where are we getting the hell to?"

"Wait one." Ferrero turned to Swift. "Where is the nearest extraction point?"

The redheaded computer tech looked up from his screen. "Six klicks to the west of their current location."

"Reaper, move six klicks west. You'll find an LZ there that's suitable for extract."

"Copy, Zero. Turning west now."

WDI Safehouse, Rio de Janeiro

A day and a half later, the team touched down and was transported to the Rio safehouse. They were tired and filthy and in need of a good shower. However, Thurston was waiting for them, her mood still on the red side.

"Get cleaned up," she said curtly. "Reaper, you're with me. Luis, you, too."

They retreated to a back room in the safehouse and closed the door. Thurston turned on Kane, her eyes narrowed and her chest heaving as she let her anger take control of her reactions. "I should kick you out on your ass right now, damn it."

"Ma'am—"

"Shut up! I'm not done speaking. I don't know what the hell you were doing disobeying direct orders like that, nor do I care." She shook her head. "Shit, of course I care. That's why we're here. Your actions put the whole team in danger, and I won't stand for it."

"Yes—"

"*Shut up!* I'm still not done. Starting right now, you are relieved of command for the duration of the mission."

"What?" Kane blurted. "You can't—"

"Am and have, damn it. You will be replaced by a man we brought in for the job."

"The hell I will," Kane growled, his anger rising.

"You brought this on yourself," Thurston replied. "I'll not stand for that kind of breach in discipline. You're lucky I'm not firing your ass."

Kane looked at Ferrero. "You agree with this?"

"It's not his decision to make," the general snarled. "It's mine. Now get the hell out before I change my mind and make it permanent."

Kane stormed out of the room and slammed the door behind him, making the walls shake. Thurston turned her hot gaze on Ferrero. "You don't agree?"

"I agree, Mary," he said. "I think it could have

been handled a little better, is all."

"Maybe it could have, but what's done is done."

Ferrero had turned to leave when the general said, "Thank you for your support, Luis. It means a lot. What happened to Kane's replacement?"

"He should be here tomorrow."

"You'll have to redirect him. Once the team has cleaned up, get them ready to move. We're joining the BOPE team."

_____

"You all right?" Cara asked Kane as he sat on a crate in the large open plan building that resembled a renovated warehouse. The entire structure was built of brick, with steel girders spanning the roof. This was the operations room. The sleeping and showering quarters were contained in two other buildings that were separated by a concrete apron from where they were now. The entire compound was surrounded by a high fence topped with razor wire. It reminded the team of a small military compound inside a foreign war zone.

Kane stopped squeezing the rubber ball he'd brought with him long enough to answer. The ball was meant to relieve tension, but at that moment, it wasn't working too well. "I will be once I get back out in the field."

"It could have been worse," Cara reminded him.

Movement caught his eye, and he saw a large man carrying a duffel enter the building. He had dark hair and a close-cropped beard. Kane shook his head. "You've got to be kidding."

"What is it?" Cara asked, her gaze following his.

"Vince 'Train Wreck' Keller. Fuck me."

"Who is he?"

"My guess is he's the new team commander."

They watched as Ferrero met him and shook hands, then the pair went to see Thurston. Cara said, "You make it sound like a bad thing."

"It is. If you go out in the field with Train Wreck, watch your six. He'll get you all killed."

"Surely it's not that bad?"

Axe appeared. "Did I see Train Wreck just now?"

"You did."

"Shit, we're all screwed."

"Take a chill pill, sweetness," Cara said to Axe. "It can't be that bad."

"Did you tell her?"

"No."

"Tell me what?"

"That Train Wreck went out with a full team and came back on his own."

"It could happen to anyone," Cara pointed out.

"Twice. What's he doing here, anyway?"

"He's the new team commander. I've been benched," Kane told him.

"Now I know we're screwed."

"Everyone, gather 'round," Thurston called.

The teams came together in the center of the room, both Reaper and Bravo. Once they were silent, Thurston continued. "This is Vince Keller. He's taking over Reaper while Kane takes a break. Make him feel welcome and show him the ropes. That means you, Cara."

"Yes, ma'am."

Keller locked gazes with Kane, then nodded. "Reaper. Been a while."

"Train Wreck."

Keller nodded. "Your team, I gather?"

"You gather right."

"Not anymore. From here on out, they're mine, and I won't take any interference from the sidelines while you're not operational. Understood?"

"Do your job right, and we won't have a problem."

An uncomfortable vibe radiated around the room. Keller moved his gaze on, and it settled on Axe. "Axelson."

"Train Wreck."

"You still an asshole?"

"Are you?"

Next, he eyed Brick. "Seems like I should know you."

"I doubt it. Brick Peters. I'm the team's combat medic."

"Always good to have one along." His gaze shifted again. "And you're Billings. My second in command."

"Yes, sir."

Troy came last. "Who are you, Tex?"

"Name's Troy, not Tex."

"We'll see."

"I guess we will."

Keller nodded and said out loud so everyone could hear, "I have high expectations, which I trust you will all live up to. If you fall out of step with them, I don't want you on my team."

"Fuck me," Axe muttered.

"Say something, Axel?" Keller glared at the man.

"Glad to have you aboard, sir."

"That's what I thought you said."

Kane glanced at Thurston, who had an angry scowl on her face. Maybe she was regretting her decision. She said, "Luis, take Keller to meet the BOPE team leader. After that, we'll have a briefing. I want to get started on locating Costa tomorrow. Axe and Reaper, you come with me."

Kane was starting to get used to getting his ass chewed, which was what he was expecting to happen now. The general took them outside and turned on them as they passed through the open doorway. "What was that?" she hissed.

"I could ask you the same thing, ma'am," Axe said insolently.

"I beg your pardon?"

"What he means, ma'am, is what the hell is Train Wreck Keller doing here?" Kane explained.

"He's here because of you, Reaper. If you hadn't gone and shot that damned French marine officer, he wouldn't need to be here."

"He *shouldn't* be here. He's a loose cannon."

Thurston's eyes widened. "Wow. Wow, wow, wow, *fucking wow.* Isn't that a bit rich coming from you at the moment, Mister Kane?"

Mister Kane. She really was pissed. She never called him that. "I stand by my comment."

"Explain."

"Have you read his record?"

"I have."

"Then you already know."

She stared at them both, her eyes burning. "Axel, I gather you feel the same way?"

"Yes, ma'am, without a doubt."

"Then I have no choice. You're sidelined too. Traynor can take your spot on the team."

"What the—" Axe started.

"This is not a democracy, gentlemen. My team, my rules. We're done."

"Ma'am—"

Thurston cut Kane off. "I said, we're done."

Both men followed her inside with their gazes. The door slammed, and Axe said, "That went well."

Kane glared at him. "You're a dick, you know that?"

"What did I do?"

"You couldn't keep your mouth shut."

"All I did was tell her the truth."

"Yes, and now you're off the team. You would have served better on it. Now Brick and Cara are on their own with that jerk."

"They've got Pete and Troy."

"You know what I mean, asshole."

Axe opened his mouth to fire back a retort, then closed it again. He nodded. "Yeah, I guess I do."

"Come on, let's see what this briefing is all about."

CHAPTER 11

Joint Taskforce Operations, Rio de Janeiro, Brazil

"This, ladies and gentlemen, is the *Vale de Perigo*, or Valley of Danger as the locals call it," Thurston said as she pointed at the screen. "It is a built-up suburb on the outskirts of Rio where even the local police don't go. Is that right, Ronaldo?"

The wide-shouldered commander of the *Batalhão de Operações Policiais Especiais* nodded. "It is true. It is one of the most dangerous places in Brazil. The only law there is the one of *matar ou morrer*. Kill or be killed."

Thurston continued. "We received intelligence that a person of interest will be there tonight."

"What person, ma'am?" Cara asked.

The screen changed, and a tall, handsome man with dark hair and a square jaw appeared. "Basilio Costa."

"Any relation to the guy we're hunting?" Keller asked.

"His brother."

"What's he doing in there?" Brick asked.

"He has a lady friend he likes to visit on a regular basis who lives there." Another picture appeared, this one of a woman who wore sunglasses, had long dark hair past her shoulders, and was well-dressed. "Lara Mota. She is a former porn star who made it big in America before returning to Brazil because her father died. It was there she met Basilio and became his mistress."

"Why is she slumming it when she could be set for life?" Brick asked.

"I guess Basilio doesn't want to upset his wife," Ferrero replied. Another picture, this woman just as attractive as the one before. "Josefa Costa. She happens to be the family lawyer."

"Why don't we pick *her* up?" Cara asked. "I'm sure she'd be a great asset."

"She already is," Ronaldo explained. "She has been turned for a while now. That is how we get our information and know about Basilio's girlfriend."

"So, the wife knows," Cara mused, raising her eyebrows.

"It would seem so," Thurston said. "Work out an assault plan with Carlos and bring it to me."

Keller got up from his seat and walked toward the screen. "Bring up the picture again."

Kane frowned. What was that asshole up to?

The new commander stared at the picture for a moment. "This is what we're going to do. We take the vehicles in, and the BOPE team sets up a defensive perimeter around the target house. My team will assault the house, take the target and his woman, and get the hell out."

"Aren't you forgetting something?" Kane spoke up. "That's the Wild West out there, and you're right in the heart of Indian country. You can't just waltz in there and expect the mission to go as smoothly as planned. We always plan the missions as a team. That way, we cover all scenarios."

"That was the way you used to do it," Keller said. "You seem to have already forgotten that this is my team now."

Kane came to his feet. "It's not your fucking team, it's mine."

"Enough!" Thurston snapped. "No more. If anyone has a right to claim this team, it is me. This is my team; I command it. If you two want to have a pissing contest about it, do it on your own time."

Kane glared at Keller. "Ma'am, how sure are we about the intel?"

"As sure as we can be. But as you know, nothing is a hundred percent."

"Request permission to go on the mission, ma'am."

"Me too, ma'am," Axe said, coming to his feet.

"Permission denied. Now, if there's nothing else,

we have a mission to prep for."

The meeting broke up. Kane contemplated going to Thurston again but knew it would do him no good. Instead, he went to Cara.

"You need to keep an eye on Keller out there, Cara. He even looks like stepping out of line, put a bullet in his head."

"Reaper—"

"I mean it. He—"

Cara dragged him toward the door by the arm. "Come with me."

"Where are we going?"

"Just do it."

They exited the ops building and walked across the concrete to the team accommodations. After opening the door to her room, she shoved Kane through and closed it behind them. "Now, tell me what this is all about."

"It's nothing. I'm just worried about the team."

Cara shook her head. "That's bullshit, Reaper. This is me you're talking to. I know you better than anyone here. What aren't you telling me?"

Kane muttered a curse as he looked into her eyes. She was right, and he knew it. He sighed. "I told you about the two missions he went out on and lost all of his command, right?"

"Yeah, right."

"The second mission was in Sierra Leone. He was leading a team of Recon Marines—"

"Wait, he was Recon?"

"Yes. Anyway, I was leading a second team. Keller came in from the south, and my team, along with Axe, was coming in from the north. Keller was supposed to wait. He didn't. Thought he could do it on his own. He walked into an ambush and got his men killed. There was nothing we could do."

"I'm sorry, Reaper. I didn't know."

He shrugged dismissively. "Yeah, well, you couldn't."

Cara reached up and touched his face, her expression softening. Her touch was gentle, and it made his heart speed up. "What...what are you doing?"

She withdrew her hand and reached down, grabbing the bottom of her T-Shirt before pulling it over her head. Beneath it, Cara wore a black bra that pushed her breasts into perfect mounds.

Kane swallowed. "Cara—"

She reached out and placed a finger on his lips. "Don't speak," she said softly before reaching back and unhooking the bra. It came loose, and she dropped it on the floor.

"I have a little time before I have to get ready. Let's not waste it."

Kane moved close and wrapped his arms around her, then stared into her eyes. "If you insist."

———

Vale de Perigo, Rio de Janeiro, Brazil

They entered the Valley of Danger in six armored SUVs—Keller, Traynor, and Troy in the first, with Cara and Brick in the second. The BOPE operators brought up the rear. Ronaldo had eight men with him. All wore masks and were heavily armed.

The slum was bathed in a silvery glow from the large, pitted moon overhead. The vehicles blew through intersection after intersection, barely slowing at each. They passed a burned-out police car, rusted where the black had washed away since it had been there that long. Only a sparse handful of streetlamps worked, their orange glow turning the streets into an eerie, desolate landscape.

Back in the second SUV, Cara watched it all slip by while Brick drove. Her trigger finger rested alongside the trigger guard, waiting for something unforeseen to happen. "I don't like it, Brick."

"What's that, ma'am?"

"There's no one out. The streets are vacant."

"Not exactly a place you'd want to venture into of a night."

"I know that but look at it. There is no one. Where was the last time you saw something like this?"

"Afghanistan when the villagers used to clear out before a Taliban attack."

"Exactly."

"They know we're coming," Brick muttered.

"Reaper Two to Reaper One, copy?"

"What is it, Reaper Two?" Keller asked abruptly.

"They know we're coming."

"Say again, Reaper Two."

"Look around you. There's no one out. The place is deserted. They know we're coming."

"You're too jumpy, Reaper Two," Keller replied. "Keep the channel clear."

"Asshole," Cara growled, then, "All call signs keep your eyes peeled. Something isn't right."

"Damn it, Reaper Two, keep off the channel," Keller said furiously.

"Reaper was right. The bastard is driving us into a fucking ambush," Cara almost screamed as she punched the glove compartment.

"Easy, ma'am," Brick said. "We'll get through this. Adapt and overcome."

She nodded. "I hope so."

Joint Taskforce Operations, Rio de Janeiro, Brazil

"What's going on?" Kane asked Thurston as he walked across the floor to the ops section.

"What are you doing here?" she asked without so much as a glance in his direction.

"I wanted to know what's happening."

Thurston glanced around the room to see who

had told Kane there was some kind of issue. "It's all fine."

Kane glanced at Arenas, who gave his head a gentle shake. He left the general's side and walked across to his friend. "What's going on, Carlos?"

"Something has Cara spooked."

"Shit." Kane grabbed a headset. "How far out from the target are they?"

"Two minutes."

"What's she spooked about?"

"I'm not sure. She said something about there not being anyone around."

Kane gave it some thought before he turned and walked over to Swift. He said, "Is all that the real-time feed?"

"Yes."

Kane stared at the screen. "Can you give me—"

"Bravo, from Reaper One, we're one minute out from the target building, over."

"Roger, Reaper One," Thurston replied. "You're one minute out."

Kane forgot what he was saying and concentrated on the ISR feed on the screen. He could see the small convoy as it sped down the rough street toward the target building.

Suddenly, the convoy split and the SUVs carrying Ronaldo and his men started to set up their defensive perimeter.

"Tiger Team moving into position," came Ronaldo's voice.

"Copy, Tiger Leader," Ferrero replied. "You are moving into position."

Kane was staring at the screen when he detected Axe beside him. "What's going on, Reaper?"

"Don't know. Cara senses something. She mentioned the streets being empty."

"Just like Afghanistan and the Taliban," Axe said offhandedly.

"Yeah, just like...shit. Teller, bring up thermal."

Overhead following the convoy's insertion into the valley was an MQ-1C Gray Eagle equipped with thermal imaging capability. Moments later, the picture on the big screen changed.

Kane stared at the screen, his jaw firm. His eyes flicked from one spot to another, mentally counting as they went.

"Sweet Jesus," he heard Axe say beside him. "They've driven into Hell."

"What are we seeing?" Thurston called.

No one answered.

"Is that the target?"

Again nothing.

"Dammit, someone talk to me!"

Kane said into his comms, "Brooke, is that Gray Eagle armed?"

"Affirmative, Reaper."

"Let's hope it's enough. Ma'am, you need to tell Keller to pull in his perimeter and fort up. He's about to get pissed on from a great height."

"Reaper One, copy?"

"Copy, Bravo. We're just pulling up to the target house now."

"Forget it. Pull your perimeter in, Reaper One. You've driven into a shitstorm."

"Say again, ma'am?"

"Pull in your perimeter. That's an order."

"Wait one—" The transmission stopped abruptly.

Everyone in the ops center looked at the screen. Small winks of heat started to appear, then the comms speakers in the room lit up. "Bravo, this is Reaper Two. We're taking heavy fire. I say again, heavy fire. Reaper One is down, possibly KIA. Please advise, over. We can't see shit from here."

Kane saw the tension on Thurston's face, but when she spoke, her orders were clear and concise. "Reaper Two, pull your perimeter in and fort up. We'll get you some help—"

Kane missed the rest because he pulled the headset off. "Axe, with me."

The pair walked over to the cage in the corner of the room where the weapons and ammunition were stored. The only things they wore when not outside the wire were their handguns.

Within minutes, Kane and Axe wore body armor and had everything else they needed, including suppressed weapons. They walked back over to where Thurston stood and Kane said, "Send us in, General."

"No."

"Damn it, General, we need to get out there."

"Just stand down for a moment, Reaper. If I send you out there now, all I'll do is get you killed. Wait and see—"

"General, we have a main-gate breach," Swift called in an urgent voice.

"Damn it, show me?"

The screen changed and showed two dark SUVs parked just inside the gates. Eight people, heavily armed and dressed in black combat gear, were exchanging fire with two BOPE shooters. A third was already down. As they watched, one of the two reacted violently to a bullet strike and joined the fallen shooter on the ground. Kane took one look and knew they were in trouble. "Come on, Axe. Time to go to work."

———————

Vale de Perigo, Rio de Janeiro, Brazil

Cara crouched behind the engine block of the SUV as a line of bullets stitched a path across its quarter panel. She muttered a curse and glanced at Brick, who was hovering over Keller. "Well?"

"He's dead, ma'am."

"Bravo, this is Reaper Two. Reaper One is KIA.

Say again, Reaper One is KIA."

"Copy, Reaper Two."

The comms went silent.

Brick looked at Cara. "What the fuck was that?"

"I don't know."

"Reaper Two, this is Tiger One. We're coming to you."

"Roger that. All Reaper call signs, covering fire."

The intensity of outgoing fire from the remaining four shooters picked up. Traynor and Troy were hunkered down behind the second SUV, which had taken the brunt of the opening fusillade.

Cara fired four evenly spaced shots at a shooter atop a roof on the opposite side of the street. Behind her, the target building was silent. It was a thin, two-story affair with a flat roof. She dropped back down and said into her comms. "Troy, Traynor, get up on top of the target building. You should get a better field of fire from there."

"Coming in!" The shout was loud over the gunfire. Ronaldo and two of his men appeared. One had been wounded.

"Where are the rest of your men?" Cara asked as a new wave of bullets smashed into the armored SUV.

"I do not know. I cannot raise them."

"All right. Everyone into the target building. Brick, when we get there, check out Ronaldo's man."

"Yes, ma'am."

Before she followed the others, Cara opened the

rear door of the SUV and took out her M110A1 CSASS, which was her preferred choice of sniper weapon. As she dragged it clear, she said, "Come to Mama, baby. You've got work to do."

Running to follow the others inside, she worked her way through the open door, speaking into her comms. "Traynor, Troy, you in position yet?"

Upstairs, the pair were running across the rooftop. "Almost, ma'am," Troy said. He looked at Traynor. "You want north and east? I'll take south and west."

"Sounds like a plan."

Troy reached the edge of the rooftop and used the parapet as a rest to commence shooting. The beam from his laser sights reached through the dark as he swept the area for targets. It wasn't long until he found one and squeezed the trigger. The 416 kicked back into his shoulder, and the figure he shot at disappeared.

Behind him, he heard footsteps, then Cara knelt beside him. "Welcome aboard, Troy. Don't forget to duck."

He fired again, using the single-shot selector on his weapon so as not to burn through too much ammunition. Cara placed her 416 on the ground and brought up the CSASS, made a couple of adjustments to it, and settled in behind the weapon. "Troy, take the west side. This street gives me a good field of fire with this—"

"RPG!"

The shout came from Traynor, who was throwing himself back from the parapet on his side. The impact of the rocket-propelled grenade rocked the building to its foundations. A bright orange flash was followed by a rising pall of black smoke.

Cara placed her weapon on the rooftop and sprinted to where Traynor lay. As she ran, she pressed the transmit button on her comms. "Brick, rooftop! Get up here *now.*"

"On my way."

Cara dropped to her knees beside Traynor, who was rolling around on his back, gasping for air. He coughed dust out of his lungs and moaned, "That was bullshit."

"Are you okay?" Cara asked hurriedly.

"I'll be all right."

Brick appeared. "What happened?"

"RPG. He took some of the blast."

A small flashlight came out of the combat medic's pocket, and he flashed it in Traynor's right eye.

"What are you frigging trying to do, blind me?" Traynor growled.

"Just keep still while I check you out."

Keeping low, Cara ran across the rooftop to where the RPG had hit. There was a big hole in the parapet, and large chunks of debris lay spread all around. She drew her handgun and peered out into the green with her NVGs. Bullets peppered her position, and she was forced to take cover. "Shit."

Lurching back to a firing position, she fired at two figures as they ran across the street below. One threw up his hands and fell to the pavement, but his friend kept going. By the looks of it, he was carrying an AK47.

"Tiger One, you've got a shooter coming in the back way."

"I have him, Reaper Two," Ronaldo responded.

"How is Pete, Brick?"

"Good to go, ma'am," came the reply through her comms.

"Get him over here."

Traynor fell in beside her. "Pete, they're trying to get in the back door. Keep them out."

"Yes, ma'am."

"Brick, you good?"

"Got my side covered, ma'am."

"Keep them out."

Cara ran back across the rooftop to retrieve her CSASS. Troy was still there, working his way steadily through the magazine he'd just loaded into the carbine. "You all right, ma'am?"

"Good to go. Take up your position."

"RPG! Northside!"

"Fuck me," Cara hissed and hugged the rooftop.

The grenade flew low across the rooftop and disappeared into the darkness of the neighborhood, terminated by a loud explosion. "I've had enough of this shit," Cara growled. "Bravo Two, copy?"

"Wait one, Reaper Two. We've got ourselves a situation. Bear with me."

"What the fuck?" Cara muttered. Here they were under heavy fire, and their main source of support was telling her to wait because they had a problem. What the hell was more important than a team in the field under siege?

CHAPTER 12

Joint Taskforce Operations, Rio de Janeiro, Brazil

"Moving!" Kane shouted as he left the cover of the Humvee, falling back behind a stack of wooden crates containing supplies. A hailstorm of bullets chased him every step of the way, eventually hammering into the boxes and chewing splinters from them.

Kane dropped out an expended magazine and replaced it with a fresh one. He rose into a crouch and fired at a shooter who sheltered behind another Humvee. The burst of fire forced the shooter down. "Axe, come to me!"

"Moving!"

Axe disengaged and dropped back to where Kane was firing, covering his retreat. Of the eight original breachers who attacked the compound, only five remained. The other three had fallen to the sudden counterattack provided by Kane and Axe. However, that hadn't lasted long. Another SUV arrived, and the attackers went to work like professionally trained killers, pushing the two Reaper men back by the weight of their fire.

"These bastards are not your average shooters, Reaper. You saw how they moved?"

More bullets chewed into the crates they sheltered behind while others cut through the air over their heads.

"Professionals," Kane allowed as he fired another burst from his 416.

More gunfire, this time from the left. Axe shifted his aim and cursed. "They're trying to flank us, Reaper."

"Well, don't let them."

Kane fired and dropped another shooter. Then he caught sight of two more who were moving right. Instinctively Kane brought his weapon around, but he was too late, and the men had made cover before he could fire. He tapped Axe on the shoulder. "We're moving again."

"After you."

"There's two shooters on the right. Watch out for them."

"Get going."

"Moving!"

Crouching, Kane ran toward the corner of the main building. Once there, he took a position and said into his comms, "Axe, come to me."

The big man stopped firing and got to his feet. Kane opened up and put out a withering cover fire. From the right, the shooters Kane had warned Axe about appeared and started firing at the running form. Kane dropped the first man with two shots. The second took one round before he lunged back behind cover, wounded but still dangerous.

"You get them?" Axe asked.

"One and clipped the other. How are you for ammo?"

Axe checked. "Two mags, one in my weapon."

"Same," Kane said.

"Reaper, sitrep, over?"

It was Thurston.

"Ma'am, we could use another shooter out here."

"On my way." A minute or so later, Thurston asked, "Where are you?"

"Corner of the building. West side."

"Coming to you."

Moments later, a figure appeared behind them, and the general made her way along the wall. When she joined them, she asked, "What have we got?"

"They pushed us back in spite of us putting a few of them down. They're professionals. The question we need to ask is who sent them?"

"Then we'd better push them back, hadn't we? Here." Thurston reached into a shoulder bag she carried and handed out fresh magazines. I figured you were low."

"Thanks, ma'am," Axe said. "I was about to go looking for a watermelon so I could spit seeds at them."

Kane and Axe dropped out partially spent magazines to reload fresh ones. Once they were done, they brought their weapons up to their shoulders. "Ready when you are, ma'am."

"Reaper, left. Axel, right. I'll go up the middle. Move."

As they broke cover, Axe gave a wry grin. "They're fucked now, Reaper. She called me 'Axel.'"

The three of them relocated using the method of move and fire. A stationary shooter was a dead shooter.

Kane felt the passage of bullets as they whipped past him. He fired at one shooter, missed, changed to another, fired, and dropped him. Then he switched back to the first one and killed him too.

Beside him, Thurston kept up a steady rate of fire, her target a big black-clad figure using a bullpup carbine. She saw one of the 5.56 caliber rounds from her 416 hit him in the chest. The man lurched under the impact and tried to steady himself. His body armor had taken the the full force. Thurston shifted her aim slightly and squeezed the trigger again. This time the big man's head snapped back as the round punched into his face.

"Argh!" On the other side of her, Axe cried out and dropped to the hard ground. She tracked across to him, firing as she went. Crouching beside Axe, she shook him. "Speak to me, Axel."

"Now you're cross at me for getting shot?" he grated.

"How bad?" she asked, firing at a shooter behind an SUV.

"Body armor took it," he replied. "I'll live."

He grunted and rolled over, picked up his weapon, and came up to one knee. "Where is that bastard?"

"Kane. Keep pressing forward," Thurston shouted.

Another shooter down, and the attackers had had enough. They disappeared through the gate into the darkness. Although not complete, a certain quiet descended over the joint taskforce compound. Kane and Axe started to check the dead. Thurston said, "We need pictures. Get one of every shooter you find. I want to know who the hell they are. If you need me, I'll be inside trying to save the rest of the team."

Vale de Perigo, Rio de Janeiro, Brazil

Another RPG sailed low over the rooftop, missing its intended target—the fifth, or maybe the sixth. Shit, Cara had lost count. "Did you see where that one came from?" she called to Troy.

"Building opposite, second-floor window," he

called back. "Same one as last time. I can't get a decent bead on the prick."

"If I can get some air—" A storm of bullets cut her short, and Cara dropped behind cover. A stinging pain bit into her cheek, and she felt the warmth of blood trickle down her face. She tried again, ignoring the burn. "If I can get some air support, we'll drop a damned Hellfire down his frigging throat."

"Ronaldo, how are you doing down there?"

"We're good. Holding our own."

"Great. How's your ammo?"

"Getting down."

"Keep me updated."

"RPG!"

It was the same asshole on Troy's side. This time the grenade clipped the top of the parapet just above where he was taking cover. The impact made it ricochet upward and keep going.

"I'm sick of this," Cara muttered. "Troy, I'm coming to you."

Cara ran across the rooftop and slid into position beside the man. "You alright?"

"I'm kind of glad that son of a bitch can't shoot for shit."

"Me too," she replied. "Get over and cover my area. I'll see if I can bag this asshole for you."

Troy retraced Cara's steps across the rooftop while she brought up the CSASS and rested it on the concrete parapet. She tucked the weapon into her shoulder, dropped her eye to the night sight, and waited, watching the window with unerring patience. Her finger rested lightly on the trigger. Normally she would rest it on the guard until she was ready to fire, but she didn't have the luxury of time. As soon as the tango with the RPG launcher appeared, she stroked the trigger.

The CSASS kicked, and its 7.62 round reached out like an airborne lance at 2,500 feet per second. Through the night sight, she saw the bullet strike and the man with the RPG launcher fall back from the open window.

"Have a nice day, motherfucker," Cara hissed angrily.

"Reaper Two, this is Bravo One, over."

About time. "Read you Lima Charlie, over."

"We've solved our situation here, over."

"Great, now you can work mine out."

"What do you need, Reaper Two?"

"Bring the rain, Bravo One," Cara replied and gave coordinates for two strikes. "Reaper Two to all call signs, keep your heads down. We have incoming ordnance."

Moments later, the neighborhood was torn apart by two loud explosions as the Hellfires impacted their targets. Giant fireballs leaped skyward and showered debris on the street below. Close enough to feel the heat wash over her, Cara had curled into a ball and was waiting for the moment to pass.

She rose to a knee to survey the damage. Two buildings had been destroyed, and what was left was burning. The gunfire had ceased, but she wasn't sure what it meant. "Brick, on me."

"Yes, ma'am."

"While they're working out what just happened, take one of Ronaldo's guys and bring Keller in."

"On it."

"Oh, and if you happen to find one of the attackers still breathing, I'd like to talk to him."

"I'll see what I can do."

_____

Joint Taskforce Operations, Rio de Janeiro, Brazil

"All right, so where are we at?"

"I'm still getting a lot of heat signatures on the ground, ma'am," Teller called. "It looks like the Hellfires worked and drove them back initially, but I think it is a short-term measure."

"How many?"

"Anywhere up to a hundred tangos still in the area of operations."

"Brooke, ordnance?"

"Still have two missiles left."

Thurston looked at her watch. "It'll be daylight soon. What is the response from the Brazilian government?"

"All we're getting is crickets, Mary," Ferrero said. "I've tried different avenues, but I'm getting nothing."

"Isn't that always the way?"

Kane stood and watched the general do her work. Even under the immense amount of pressure bearing down upon her, she remained cool and collected.

"Ma'am," said Swift. "I've got an ID on one of the shooters who attacked the compound."

"Show me."

A picture appeared. The man was wearing a military uniform. "Michael Walters. Former British Commando. Served six years before being recruited by MI6. After that, he's a ghost."

"Seem to be a lot of them around lately," Thurston breathed. "All right, Slick, keep digging."

"Yes, ma'am."

"Reaper Two, sitrep."

"General, we're a little banged up, but we're still in the fight. We have one WIA and one KIA. Both have now been secured. We also have six MIA."

Thurston paused momentarily. "Status on your wounded?"

"WIA is priority three. Over."

"What about your transport?"

"Transport is screwed."

"All right, Reaper Two. Hang in there. We're trying to get you some help. Out."

Thurston turned to Kane. "You and Axe get reprovisioned. Take whatever you need to break through. Extra ammo, grenade launchers—hell, if Cara has a damned tank hidden back there somewhere, take it too. Just get through to them and get them out."

"What about the MIAs, ma'am?"

Thurston thought for a moment before turning to her UAV team. "Teller, how far have the tangos pulled back?"

"Outside the original defensive perimeter, ma'am."

She nodded. "Reaper Two, copy?"

"I'm still here, Bravo."

"According to ISR, your friends have pulled back beyond the originally planned perimeter. Send out a two-man patrol and see if you can find your missing. We'll provide overwatch."

"Roger that, Bravo. I'll get right on it."

"Understand this, Reaper Two. You're in command. Do not go yourself."

"Understood, ma'am. Reaper Two, out."

"Was that necessary, General?" Kane asked.

Thurston stared at him. "What are you still doing here? I gave you an order. Move."

"Yes, ma'am."

———

Rio de Janeiro, Brazil

Grayson wasn't happy. The attack on the compound had been unsuccessful, and her team had let her down. Well, it wouldn't happen again. Next time, and there would be a next time, she would send more of everything. She turned away from the hotel window and stared at Flint. "What about the ambush set up by Basilio Costa?"

"There is some kind of hiatus. They were on top of the situation, and then they were hit with missiles from a UAV, and it took the sting out of the attack."

"Is there anything that Basilio needs? If we can keep him pressing the attack, we can still salvage something from the fire."

"He is a proud man. I have asked, and he refuses anything which might leave him more beholden to you than he already is."

"Maybe we should help him anyway. Spin up the AC-130. Let's give him a little something on the house."

"Yes, ma'am."

"Redeploy some of our men. They can organize the ground forces. We'll win this thing yet."

Flint left the room, and Grayson walked toward the door at the other end of the suite she occupied. She stopped when she reached the sofa. Undoing the buttons on her black blouse, she removed it, revealing a white camisole beneath. She then took off her pants, leaving on her lacy black panties. It would be easier this way—less mess.

Grayson continued her journey toward the door and paused only momentarily to open it. The door swung wide to reveal a man, completely naked, tied to a chair in the center of the room. His face was a bloody mess, as were the stumps on his right hand where two of his fingers had been removed. The blood had dripped onto the clear plastic that covered the floor. Stuffed into the man's mouth was a bloody gag.

"Did you miss me, Alfredo?" Grayson asked politely.

Alfredo Costa grunted, his nostrils flaring as he anticipated what was to happen next. "I believe we were talking about a little matter to do with the money you've hidden away. Your brother is paying me well to get rid of you, but a little more earned on the side... Well, let's just say I would put it to good use."

Alfredo grunted and snorted around the gag in his mouth. Grayson pouted playfully. "You have something to say, poor baby?" She removed the gag.

"Fucking prostitute. Kill me and get it over with."

"Tell me about the money."

He spat at her, and the globule landed between her milky white breasts and ran down her cleavage. Grayson shrugged. "Oh, well."

She put the gag back into the cartel boss' mouth

and walked to the small table in the corner of the room, her bare feet making the plastic crinkle. On the surface of the table rested implements used for various forms of torture. Grayson let her hand hover above them before making her decision and picking up the scalpel. She held it in front of her eyes, which glinted wickedly like the razor-sharp blade in the false light. Her lips peeled back from her white teeth in a vicious smile. "Perfect."

Grayson turned back to Alfredo and walked around so she was facing him. "Where should I start this time? Do you have a preference?"

The beads of sweat on his brow came instantly. She smiled at him. "Take it easy, love. I promise I'll be gentle." Her eyes wandered down his body to his groin. The chair seat was built to accommodate a commode, the hole vacant. His legs were tied to the chair legs on either side. Grayson stepped forward and traced a finger over the drug lord's hairy chest. He strained at the ropes, his efforts forcing out animalistic grunts.

The hand sank until it reached his crotch. It paused to stroke his flaccid cock until it started to harden, rebelling against the terrified man's wishes. Within moments it was fully engorged, which brought another smile to Grayson's lips. "Wow, you were at the front of the line when they handed them out, weren't you?"

Alfredo's grunts and breathing grew swifter and

his efforts more desperate. Grayson stopped strok-
ing him and moved her hand lower until it cupped
his balls. Again, the smile, this time mirthless, cold.
She held the scalpel up for him to see. "You've had
children, haven't you?"

She lowered it, and with the first stroke, Alfredo's
eyes bulged, and he screamed into the gag.

———————

The sun was up by the time Grayson had finished.
She took a shower to wash off Costa's blood, then
walked naked into the main room of the suite. The
muscles on her well-toned body rippled with every
step. If she was surprised to see Flint there, she
didn't show it. She just said, "He told me where he
has hidden two hundred and fifty million. I want
you to take a team to retrieve it."

Flint nodded. This wasn't the first time he'd seen
her naked, but the sight still did something to him.
She noticed and walked over to the large plate-glass
window she'd been standing at earlier.

His eyes followed her, watching her tight buttocks as they undulated with each step. The heart
they formed was almost perfect.

Grayson placed her hands on the window, spread
apart at shoulder height. "Come here, Ben."

He swallowed and walked forward, then stood
behind her and waited. She said, "Do it."

Flint unbuckled his pants and let them fall to his ankles. He stepped closer, and Grayson adjusted her position to accept him. As he entered her, he thrust hard. Grayson threw her head back and moaned. By the time Flint was finished, his boss was screaming in ecstasy as all of the sexual tension from the torture of Alfredo Costa poured out of her.

Flint stepped back, his face bathed in sweat. He pulled up his pants and zipped them. Grayson turned to face him, her face as red and sweaty as his was. Her bangs were wet and matted to her forehead. She angrily said, "Get out."

CHAPTER 13

Vale de Perigo, Rio de Janeiro, Brazil

Troy edged up to the end of the building and paused. Before he stuck his head around the corner, he listened. No point in sticking your head out if some bastard was going to put a bullet in it. Behind him was Traynor. Both had been tasked with finding their MIAs. So far, they were out of luck, but according to the directions they'd been given, around the corner would be one of the SUVs used by the BOPE operators. He glanced at Traynor, who was looking the other way, watching for threats in that direction.

Troy eased his head around the corner of the building, trying not to expose himself too much, and saw the SUV. It was a burned, blackened ruin. Beside it were three bodies that had been stripped bare, their skin stark white in the morning sun.

Troy drew back and looked at Traynor. "Looks

like we've found three of them."

Traynor moved around him and looked for himself. "Shit."

He eased around the corner while Troy took up rear security. They stepped onto the street, and already they could smell the fumes from the SUV.

They checked the corpses to make sure, not that there was any doubt. "Reaper Two, this is Traynor. We've located three of our guys. They're all deceased, over."

"Roger that. Circle back to the east and then come in, over."

"Copy."

"Wait," Troy said. "Hear that?"

"What?" Traynor asked.

It was a low droning sound, far off but getting closer. "It's a plane."

Traynor nodded. "Big plane."

With a loud roar, the winged beast appeared low overhead. "Good grief!" Troy exploded.

"We've got to get back."

"Reaper Two, get off the rooftop," Troy almost shouted into his comms as he started to run. "Get off now!"

_____

Cara looked up as the gunship was making its approach. Then her comms lit up, and a cold hand gripped her heart. "Fuck me. *Brick, get off the rooftop! Now!*"

She started running for the stairwell, Brick followed close behind her. In the sky, the gunship had already started its banking turn. Then it opened fire.

The impact of the first round and the resulting explosion rocked the building, throwing Cara and Brick against the wall in the stairwell. She cried out as pain shot through her left shoulder. Dust rained down, but they gathered themselves and kept going.

"They can't have hit it," Brick shouted. "Or we'd be dead about now."

At the foot of the stairs, they were met by Ronaldo. "We've got to go," Cara gasped, not slowing down.

She burst out into the dust-shrouded sunshine with Brick, Ronaldo, and the remaining two BOPE men following her. The roar of the plane filled their ears, and the world was torn apart as a round from the 105mm main armament inside the AC-130's guts smashed into the target house.

The explosion knocked them all flat on the street. Cara winced as a large piece of masonry hit her in the middle of the back, her body armor taking the full force of the blow. She cried out in pain, twisting as she tried to escape it. Brick crawled to her. "Are you all right, ma'am?"

"Just get me under cover," she growled.

"Hang on."

Instead of carrying her, he grabbed the strap on her webbing and dragged her unceremoniously across the street and behind a battered old vehicle.

"Where does it hurt, ma'am?"

"My back."

Brick rolled Cara over while Ronaldo and his men kept watch. The AC-130 fired at the target building again, this time obliterating it.

Brick dropped flat over Cara, who cried out as his weight crashed down on top of her. "You trying to kill me too?" she moaned.

"Sorry, ma'am. Old habits."

He managed to loosen her body armor and lift her garments. The bruise on her back was already distinguishable. He pressed around it, eliciting a hiss of pain. "I think you'll be all right, ma'am, but you'll have one hell of a bruise."

"Reaper Two, sitrep, over?"

"Not now, Bravo."

"Say again, Reaper Two."

The gunship fired again, and a house across the street exploded.

"Ma'am, we've got a damned Specter on-station, and it's blowing the crap out of everything. If you can't help, leave me alone until I can get us out of the damned fix you got us into. Out."

She looked at Brick, who smiled. "You'll be fine, ma'am."

Cara sat up. "Give me my damned weapon, and let's get back into this fight."

"What do you propose we do?"

"I have no shitting idea."

Kane and Axe drove through the rundown neighborhood as though the hounds of hell were chasing them. Kane was behind the wheel of the armored Humvee and Axe was standing up in the back, manning the fifty-caliber machine gun. Before they left, Kane had thought about taking one of the remaining SUVs, but they were beyond that, and from the reports coming in from the operations area, the fifty was a good choice.

The Humvee leaped over a hump in the street before Kane jammed on the brakes and turned hard right. In the turret, Axe tried to brace himself, but his ribs found the edge, and he let out a grunt of pain. "You trying to kill me before we get there, Reaper?"

"Just shut up and hang on."

"Getting there in one piece would be a start, amigo," Arenas said from the passenger seat. When Kane and Axe were about to leave, they had been approached by Arenas, armored up and ready for war.

Above the buildings rose two palls of smoke. Above that and doing tight circles was the Specter.

"Get me into position, Reaper," Axe called. "I always wondered what one of these things would do to a plane."

"Just don't miss or you're screwed."

They motored into the war zone. Kane took a right, then a left, followed by another right.

"Reaper Two, copy?"

"Read you Lima Charlie, Reaper."

"Sitrep, over."

"That Specter is—" The transmission stopped.

"Say again, Reaper Two."

"We're getting the shit kicked out of us by that damned plane. Over."

"We're coming in from the west. Hold tight."

"We're doing everything we can to hold on, Reaper."

The Humvee broke out of an alley into the open area near an intersection. Everything around it was a scene of destruction and devastation. Across the street where the target building had been was a blackened, burning pile of rubble. After that had been destroyed, another three buildings had been hammered as well.

Kane pulled the Humvee close to one of the buildings that still stood to try to keep one side of the vehicle away from the circling AC-130, not that it would count for much. A 105mm shell in the right place, and they were done for anyway.

"Wait until it comes around again and give it everything, Axe," Kane ordered.

The Specter disappeared behind them, and an explosion rocked the block. Axe said, "What the hell are they shooting at?"

"I don't know. Reaper Two, are they dialed in on your position?"

"Negative. They're looking for us."

"All right, keep your head down."

The gunship came back around, and as soon as he could get a clear shot, Axe opened fire with the fifty. The weapon's deep-throated *chug-chug* echoed around the intersection as small ballistic missiles arced skyward, their path marked by the glow of tracer rounds.

Axe cursed as he watched them all fall behind the plane.

"*Amigo*, you shoot like shit," Arenas growled.

"Shut up!" Axe shouted above the noise of the gun.

The Specter opened fire with its rotary cannon and the area around the Humvee was ripped apart, the ground exploding upward. "You'd better get that thing now or we're all fucked, Axe," he called.

"I'm trying, damn it."

"Try harder."

"There you go, riding my ass again," Axe growled. His face hardened into granite as he willed the rounds from the heavy machine gun to hit their target. "Blaming me for all the shit you get us into and expecting me to get you out. Axe, do this. Axe, do that. How about you do some of this shit yourself?"

"Have you got it yet?"

"Shut up."

Huge lumps of masonry fell from the building behind them as round after round from the rotary canon punched into it, making it seemingly explode. Then, faint at first before becoming a dark trail, smoke emerged from one of the AC-130's engines.

"Take that, asshole!" Axe yelled in frustration as the gun ran dry.

The trail of smoke from the Specter got thicker and darker, then a flash lit the sky and the engine exploded, shearing off the wing and rendering the machine unflyable.

It hung there for a moment before the metal beast crashed to earth in a ball of orange flame and black smoke.

"Reaper Two, give me your position, over."

Cara told him where they were.

"I'll be there in a moment. Out."

———————

Rio de Janeiro, Brazil

"We lost the Specter," Flint said as he put his cell back into his pocket.

Grayson glared at him. "What happened? And why aren't you looking for the money?"

"It got shot down. And the money can wait. I thought this was more important."

"Shot down? How?" Her voice was filled with surprise.

"Lucky shot from a fifty-caliber machine gun."

"What about the team on the ground?"

"As far as we know, they are still holding out and have been joined by reinforcements," Flint explained.

"What about our men? Have they arrived on-site yet?"

"They should be getting there about now."

"How many of them?"

"Six."

"Keep me updated."

"Do you want to move location?" Flint asked her.

She looked toward the room where Alfredo Costa still sat tied to the chair, dead. "We'll move to the secondary location."

"And him?" he asked, indicating the closed door.

"Leave him."

"Yes, ma'am."

Vale de Perigo, Rio de Janeiro, Brazil

Cara limped over to Kane. She and the others had emerged from a partially destroyed building that was formerly two floors but now had one. She looked around and shook her head. "It looks like Afghanistan."

Brick had blood on the side of his face, which was covered in a fine powder. The three BOPE operators, including Ronaldo, were battered and bleeding as well. "Where's Traynor and Troy?" Kane asked.

"They were outside the wire looking for MIAs when the Specter came in. The last I heard was them telling us to get off the rooftop."

"Are you alright?" Kane asked her, seeing the pain etched in her face.

"Nothing a Caribbean holiday with some hunk pampering me wouldn't fix," she grumbled.

"I'll see if Axe is free."

"Asshole."

"I've got movement, Reaper," Axe said from the turret of the Humvee. He pointed the reloaded fifty in the direction of the threat to show them where.

Kane and Cara turned and saw two men stumble out of a rubble-littered alley. They were dirty, and their clothes almost white from stucco dust. Their faces were painted much the same way, but there was no mistaking their identity. The ballistic helmets and weapons they carried gave that away. "Hold fast, Axe," Cara said. "It's Traynor and Troy."

The two operators limped across the open intersection and stopped in front of the others. Cara said, "You both look like crap."

Traynor shook his head. "That was some intense shit."

Troy spat blood. Somewhere along the way, he'd been hit in the mouth by something, and his teeth had cut the inside of his lips. "I'm done with you, Reaper. Every time I do something for you, it almost gets me killed."

"What, can't handle the excitement?"

He spat blood once more. "I can do without—"

THWAP! Troy grunted and slumped to the street.

"Shooter across the street!" Axe shouted, and the fifty began its familiar rhythm.

"Shit," Kane snarled and dragged Troy behind the Humvee.

Cara acted on instinct and muscle memory; she turned and brought up the CSASS. The scope came to her eye as she sought the target. She was guided by the storm of heavy machine-gun fire from Axe. Holes appeared in the wall where the rounds struck, big enough to put a fist through.

Whereas the fifty was a blunt instrument, the sniper system was a surgical weapon, and one shot was all it would take to silence the shooter. Cara squeezed the trigger, and the weapon kicked back into her shoulder with the comfort of an old friend. The projectile reached out and struck the shooter in the head, a red mist spraying the air when the round blew out the back.

It was as though the kill was a signal to unleash

hell upon the team. Now that the threat of the Specter was neutralized, Basilio Costa's soldiers moved in once more, led by Grayson's men, to take up the fight.

Cara dived behind the Humvee as bullets cut through the air. Meanwhile, above her, Axe had the fifty thumping a familiar tune. She looked across at Kane and Troy. "Is he alright, Reaper?"

"Body armor took the impact."

Troy winced. "Hurts like a son of a bitch, but I'm good."

Bullets peppered the Humvee as the team sent more outgoing rounds at their attackers. Even with the Specter gone, things hadn't improved.

"Reaper!" Axe called. "Shooters moving left to flank. You need to block them before they get in behind us."

Kane tapped Brick on the shoulder and said, "Come on, sunshine. Work to do."

The pair broke cover, racing for an alley that would lead them to the rear of the target house or what was left of it. As he went, Kane called the ops center. "Bravo One, copy?"

"Copy, Reaper."

"I need to know what's happening on the ground."

"Wait one."

Kane and Brick reached the alley. It was littered with debris and rubble, which made their progress slower than they would have liked. Kane stumbled over a lump of masonry and caught himself before he fell. However, the stumble made him vulnerable, and at that moment a shooter chose to appear, weapon raised to fire. He could do nothing to stop it.

Brick though, was alert and fired twice. The killer jerked under each strike and fell to the ground. "Thanks," Kane growled.

They traversed the alley and reached the end where the shooter had fallen. His face was covered in tattoos, and he had gold chains around his neck. On his forearm was a string of small knives, which Kane thought might indicate his kills.

Brick checked the street and saw that it was empty. Abandoned cars were parked hap-hazard at odd angles, doors open where people had fled them. "This isn't right," Brick said.

"What isn't?"

"These vehicles. When we came into the valley, it was like a ghost town. Everything was deserted."

"Reaper One. Copy?"

"Copy, Bravo One."

"We're seeing a buildup of activity to the southwest behind where the target building used to be."

Brick looked at Kane. "I guess we know which way they're coming from."

"Right down this street."

"Also, Reaper, I've been advised to order you out of the valley, over."

"Who by?"

"The mayor of Rio."

"The mayor? Did I hear you right?"

"Roger that. Apparently, he was unaware of our presence and now that he knows, isn't happy about it."

"What is the government saying about it?"

"Nothing. They're incommunicado."

"Shit," Kane growled. "You tell me how I'm supposed to get everyone out of here with one vehicle and a damned army on its way."

"I'm just the messenger, Reaper."

Brick tapped Kane on the shoulder. "That army you were talking about is already here."

Kane looked down the street and saw them advancing. A large armed force spread from one side to the other. "Do you still have that UAV up, Bravo One?"

"We've been ordered to take it off-station."

"If you take it off-station, we're all dead."

"I'm sorry, Reaper."

Kane's anger grew. If they took the Gray Eagle away, his team would be overrun. They needed the Hellfires. "Bravo One, I think your UAV is too heavy and might crash if you don't lighten the load. I suggest you jettison your payload before it falls into a built-up neighborhood."

"You could be right, Reaper One. Jettisoning payload. Keep your head down."

"Reaper One to all call signs. We have incoming

ordnance. Make yourselves small."

When they came, the two explosions rocked the neighborhood to its core. The ground vibrated and shook, and some of the vehicles on the street were caught in the blast. The sudden violence took the fight out of the advancing crowd and left bodies everywhere. Kane and Brick pulled back to the others. Cara met him and asked, "What's happening?"

"We've been ordered out."

"How? Are they sending something for us?"

Kane shook his head. "Not as far as I know."

"So, how?"

"We walk."

CHAPTER 14

Joint Taskforce Operations, Rio de Janeiro, Brazil

"Okay, talk to me," Thurston said.

"Kane and the others are walking out on foot," Ferrero said. "We just dropped our last two Hellfire missiles on top of an advancing hostile crowd."

The general's head snapped around. "What? How did that happen?"

"Well—"

Thurston turned. "Brooke, what happened?"

Reynolds turned her head from her console. "I'll be happy to have that conversation, ma'am, just as soon as I land the UAV."

"It's a simple question."

"The crowd was close to the team and could have overrun them. Reaper thought he saw that the UAV was in danger of crashing into a populated neighborhood and suggested that I lose some weight before it crashed."

"He did, did he?"

"Yes, ma'am. Will there be anything else?"

"No. The rest can wait." She turned back to Ferrero. "How could you have let this happen? I've been on the phone trying to sort this mess out, and now I find out we've dropped two hundred pounds of ordnance."

"Better to do it now and apologize later, Mary. If it hadn't been done, the team would have been overrun. It was the only option we had to have any chance of keeping them alive."

"I'll be the judge of that," she snapped.

Behind them, Swift cleared his throat. They both turned, and Thurston glared at him. "What?"

"I thought you might like to know that forty-five minutes ago, Alfredo Costa was found dead in a hotel suite downtown. He'd been tortured."

"Keep talking."

"Reports are that a cleaner found him tied to a chair. His testicles had been removed, among other things."

"Do they have any idea who did it?"

Swift was holding a piece of paper and tapping it on the palm of his opposite hand. "I managed to hack into the hotel's files and cameras and came up with this."

He handed what he held to the general. Thurston looked at it, then passed it to Ferrero. He in turn studied it, then looked at the computer tech. "It's her."

"It looks like it."

"We still don't know who she is." It was a statement.

"Not yet, but I managed to put names to two more of the shooters who attacked our compound."

"Who?"

"John Goddard and Robert Slater. One was former SBS, and the other served with the British Sixteen Air Assault Brigade."

Thurston said, "Is it just me, or is there some kind of pattern here?"

"I'm seeing it," Ferrero agreed. "Search the British databases and see if you can come up with something, especially the Security Service and Secret Intelligence Service. Reach out to any contacts you have. Someone must know something."

"Yes, sir."

The anger was gone from Thurston when she turned to Ferrero. "What do you suppose she wanted with Alfredo Costa?"

"If it were a straight assassination, I would say someone paid her to do it. Torture was more personal, or—" He paused.

"What?"

"Or she wanted something."

"I'll bite. What?"

"What does a drug boss have plenty of?"

"Drugs and money."

Ferrero nodded. "From what little we know about her I don't think she's the drugs type."

"So, it's money?"

"I'd say so. We know Costa has, or had, a lot of it. Some in cash-stash locations. It's just a matter of finding out where they are. To do that—"

"Torture would help," Thurston finished. "But doing something like that to the biggest drug cartel leader in Brazil took some balls."

"Unless you have a brother who wants to take over."

"So he gets her to kill him. But why would he want his brother tortured?"

"I don't think the orders came from him. I'd say our ghost saw an opportunity and took it."

The general nodded. "All right, I'll buy that. But those assholes who attacked our compound. You think they're linked?"

"It's a hunch I have. I'm assuming she's a gun for hire. She comes down here for one job and ends up doing two."

Thurston nodded. "But which job did she come here for?"

"That is the million-dollar question."

"We need to find out who that bitch is."

"You're not wrong there. In the meantime, we have to work out what to do with Kane and the others."

"Give me a moment, and I'll make a call."

"Yes, ma'am."

Five minutes later, she put in a call to Kane and the others. "Reaper One, copy?"

"Read you Lima Charlie, Bravo."

"I've pulled a couple of strings and managed to get a helo for your extract. What happened to the Humvee?"

"All vehicles were put out of commission, ma'am. Axe is humping the fifty."

"Roger that. There's an area large enough for an LZ about one klick to your south. Move the team there and make contact."

"Roger."

"Kane?"

"Yes, ma'am?"

"What happened to Keller?"

"He's buried under two floors of rubble, General. Nothing we could do about that."

"I'll see if I can work something out to get him back. Bravo out."

———————

The team made the rendezvous without further incidents. The last two Hellfire missiles had taken all the fight out of Basilio Costa's men. However, it hadn't done so for the mayor of Rio, who was demanding that they all leave his city, or they would be arrested.

When the team returned to the compound, they

went straight to Doc Morales for examinations. Once they were done and cleared, they gathered in the ops center for debriefing. Cara was still in pain from the hit to her back, as was Troy from the round in his body armor. In one way or another, each team member required some form of attention.

"You all look like shit," Thurston said.

"Yeah, well…" Cara said.

Kane gave her a sideways glance, and that was all it took for him to recognize what was coming.

The general said, "If you've got something to say, do it now."

"All right, I will. That bullshit out there could have been fucking avoided." There was fire in Cara's eyes. Some came from the burning pain in her back, but most of it was from the anger she felt. "You were told what Keller was like. He just came in here, threw his weight around, and completely fucked up when all he had to do was consult with us. He almost got us all killed in the process, mind you. That is on you, General."

"Are you done?" Thurston asked.

Kane stepped forward. "Hold up. If you want to blame someone, blame me. If I hadn't done what I did, this would never have happened."

Cara turned her hot gaze on him. "I'll get to you later."

Kane held up both of his hands and took a step back.

She turned her stare back on the general. Thurston nodded. "All right, I'll wear it. Not my finest hour, and I apologize for it. But now we've got to move on, so if anyone else wants to get something off their chest, do it now. I won't tolerate it later."

Axe put his hand up.

Thurston's eyes narrowed. "Except you."

"I was just going to ask if we've had news about Knocker?"

"Nothing as yet."

Silence.

Thurston sighed. "All right then, let me bring you up to speed with what's happening. First off, we're under orders from the mayor to get out of the city. For the time being, I've chosen to ignore those orders, but I can't for too long. Secondly, the lay of the land has changed somewhat. This morning while you all were out playing with the natives, Alfredo Costa was found tortured to death in a hotel suite rented by this woman."

The team looked at the picture on the screen. By now, she was familiar.

"That's her, isn't it?" Axe asked.

"Yes. Our friend from Chechnya. The one we've been trying to track."

"What's she doing here?"

"We have a theory," Ferrero answered. "We think she came here for one job and ended up with two. Right now, we're trying to work out what her primary was."

"I get that she killed Costa," Kane said. "It has all the hallmarks of a hostile takeover, but why torture him?"

"Money," the former DEA agent said, rubbing his fingertips together in the universal sign. "Costa was known to have cash stashed everywhere."

"If he was one mission, that would make us the second," Cara theorized.

"The attack on the compound pretty much confirmed that. Plus, every one of the dead we've been able to identify is former British military."

Troy said, "Wait up. Have the Brit military records been checked for the woman's identity? If the guys who work for her are Brits, surely she is too."

"I've checked and come up blank," Swift said.

"What about their security services?"

"Yes, nothing there either."

"What about their black ops?"

"Yes, *nada*."

"What's the matter, Troy?" Kane asked.

"Something doesn't add up. The woman is a ghost, which says she has training. She can live in plain sight without triggering anything like facial recognition and other red-flag security measures. She's a Brit—best guess—and she runs her people like a military officer. Throw in that she's not afraid to get her hands dirty, and she has spook written all over her. So why can't you find her in the Security Service files?"

"Because she's either dead or disavowed," Cara said, leaning forward in her seat.

"Shit, shit, fuck!" Thurston growled, drawing all eyes in the room toward her.

"Something wrong, Mary?" Ferrero asked.

"We've all been thinking it, Luis. Is it too much to hope they've gone away?"

"I gather you're talking Cabal?"

"Who do we know that was Security Service, head of special operations, and high up in the Cabal?"

"She's dead, Mary."

"No, we *think* she's dead. You know what those bastards are like."

"But we froze all their accounts. They've got no access to money."

"That we know of. Everything we've tied her to of late ran into big dollars. We know how much the Yakuza paid and killing Costa would have paid a pretty penny too. She tortured him to find out where he hid his money, and then there was the attack on our compound. The bitch is building up a bank account to bring the Cabal back out of the darkness. The question is, who would pay the amount of money she would command to take us off the board?"

"That could be anyone from a hundred different countries," Brick said.

"I can think of someone," Cara said. "Gustaw Marek."

"You think he's crawled out of his hole?" Ferrero asked.

"We always knew he would. Maybe he's got the money to do it."

"I just thought of something," Kane said. "What if she's behind Knocker going missing? If she's after all of us, why not him too?"

Thurston shook her head. "Knocker wasn't with us when we took down Marek's empire. No, his disappearance has something to do with what he's working on."

"I suppose you're right."

"I could be wrong, too. Slick, do you feel up to juggling a couple of things?"

"It's what I do best," the redheaded tech announced proudly.

"Look into Mosul. Find anything you can that might help. Also, I need a surveillance package for the op tonight."

"Yes, ma'am."

"What op?" Kane asked.

"We're going after Basilio Costa. We have intel that he has a meeting tonight at a club he owns in downtown."

Kane looked at his team. "They're in no shape for an op tonight, ma'am."

"Agreed. That's why it'll be you and Brooke. You

go in, neutralize the target, and get out."

"It's a hit?"

"Yes. Do you have a problem with that?"

Kane knew what she was getting at. "No problem, ma'am. What will we have for backup?"

"Oh, no. You don't get backup. This time you're on your own. This thing is off the books." She looked at her watch. "As of five minutes ago, we're not even in this country."

"Fuck."

_____

Luzes da Cidade Nightclub, Rio de Janeiro, Brazil

As Kane and Reynolds joined the long line of party-goers, she leaned close to Kane and whispered into his ear, "I've never felt more exposed."

He grinned. "You mean the dress or the lineup?"

"Both."

Reynolds wore a short black dress that barely covered her buttocks. The neckline plunged just below her navel. The swell of her breasts was exposed, and the fabric only just covered her nipples. Her long dark hair hung down her back, and the earrings and makeup she wore had her looking somewhere between high-class and a high-class hooker. Kane said, "Can I ask you a question?"

"What?"

"Where the hell have you got your gun?"

"Don't ask. It's easy for you."

This was true. Kane wore a T-Shirt and jeans, so hiding his weapon had been easy. The only problem was getting past security, but BOPE had seen to that by putting one of their UCs on the door. Supposedly.

The line crept closer to the main doors, with each reveler being checked before they entered. Kane looked at his watch. They'd been in line for around twenty minutes, and judging by the speed it was going, it would be at least another twenty.

"You," a heavily accented voice called.

Natural instinct told him to look in the direction it came from, but Kane kept his eyes fixed straight ahead.

"You," the voice said again. This time, however, it was more demanding.

Kane looked to his left and saw a thickset man wearing a suit staring at him. "You talking to me?"

He nodded. "Yes. You and her. Come with me."

Kane glanced at Reynolds. "What do you think?"

She shrugged. "What can go wrong?"

"You've spent way too much time with Axe."

She smiled at him. "Come on, honey. Let's see what the nice man wants."

They stepped out of line and joined the man, who waited for them on the pavement. Under the streetlamp, Kane could see the sweat on the man's brow, which reminded him about the humidity of the night air. The man nodded and said, "Follow me."

He took them past the line to the main doors, where two armed men stood blatantly not concealing their MAC-10 machine pistols. They stepped aside and let them through, and no attempt was made to search them.

Inside the place was jumping. The music was loud, and sweaty bodies were jammed together. Many of the guys inside were without shirts, and the women seemed to have discarded theirs as well. Reynolds leaned close to Kane's ear. "I feel overdressed."

They were taken into a small, sterile room. There was nothing on the walls, no cameras, just two chairs and a metal desk. Kane tensed. "What are we doing in here? What's going on?"

The man said, "I will make this quick. Basilio Costa is in the far-right corner of the club, meeting with a woman. They both have bodyguards and—"

"How many?" Kane asked.

"Two each."

"The woman has six," Reynolds corrected.

The man's brow furrowed. "What?"

"There is no way she would come in here with only two guards. I made out two near the dancefloor on the way in here."

The man looked at Kane, who nodded. "If she says six, there are six. How many more shooters does Costa have?"

"Two with him, two outside, and two more at

the bar."

"Bullshit."

Once more, their insider was surprised by the response. Kane continued. "This is his place. There is no way he has only six shooters here."

The man's eyes darted toward the closed door as he licked his lips with a nervous look on his face. Suddenly Kane realized why he was sweating so much. They'd walked into a trap. "Shit!" he growled and drew his weapon from behind his back. "Prepare for incoming, Brooke."

Kane placed the barrel of the M17 against the forehead of the startled man. "They know, don't they."

"Know what?" he asked in a high-pitched voice.

Kane put his hand to his earbud. "Bravo, we've walked into a trap."

"Copy, Reaper. What's the plan?"

He looked at Reynolds, who now had her weapon in her hand. She nodded, answering the unspoken question. Kane said, "We're going for the target. Be advised this may be a strikeout."

"Negative, Reaper. Advise you to withdraw. We can do this another day."

Kane thought for a moment. "Wait one, ma'am."

He reached into his pocket and took out his cell, then flicked through it until a picture of the mysterious woman appeared. He turned it so the man who'd brought them to the room could see it. "Is this the woman he's with?"

The man said nothing, just stared at the cell. Kane lifted his handgun again and pressed it hard to the man's head. "Answer the fucking question."

The man nodded. "Yes, yes. That is her."

"Bravo, we have confirmation that there are two targets on-site. One of them is the woman."

"Are you sure?"

"Not until I lay eyes on her."

"It's up to you, Reaper."

"We're going for it. Reaper out."

"Reaper," Reynolds said, "there is the slight problem of a packed dancefloor."

"That's why we need to separate them."

"How?"

"I have a plan."

———————

Kane followed the man through the crowd as he led him toward where Costa and the others were seated in the far corner of the room. The man had taken some convincing, but he'd been persuaded after a couple of minutes.

Basilio Costa saw them coming and straightened in his seat. He removed his arm from around a woman Kane recognized as the porn actress he was seeing on the side. He said something, and the woman opposite him turned her head. Kane recognized her. Ellen Grayson was alive and well. He mumbled under his breath, "Bravo, I have eyes on Ellen Grayson, over."

"Copy, Reaper. You have eyes on Ellen Grayson."

He stopped short of the table and glanced at the people staring at him. Two were white males. He guessed they were Brits, part of the bodyguard detail for Grayson. The other two were with Costa. Then there was the mistress, who he'd already figured out.

The fire alarm sounded, and the music stopped. The DJ started directing the patrons toward the fire doors, urging them to go calmly. Soon the club was empty of patrons and staff. The only ones left were Costa, Grayson, and the bodyguards—all ten of them.

Costa said, "I was told you would not be able to resist. It seems I was told right."

"How's your brother?" Kane asked. "Last I heard, he was a little cut up."

"It is what it is," Costa said nonchalantly.

"Those hostile takeovers can be a real bitch," Kane stated. "Speaking of which, how are you, Ellen? Long time no see."

"Mister Kane. I'm glad you could join us. I've a lot of money at stake with your team."

"Trying to get the old gang back together, Ellen?"

She gave him a cold smile. "The old gang never went away. I do wish we had more time to catch up, but you know how it is."

"I guess so. Although I'm interested in who paid all that money to have you take us off the board. We thought it might have been Gustaw Marek."

"He really doesn't like you. Did you know that?"

"Yeah, kind of comes with the territory of killing his son."

"He's willing to part with fifty million."

"Wow, there's a lot of hate there." Kane shook his head, considering the contract.

"Yes, I got a lot less for Knocker."

Kane's blood ran cold. "Knocker? Knocker wasn't with us when we hit Marek."

"No, he wasn't, was he? That's why our friendly neighborhood Ghost has him."

It felt like a blow to the guts, but he wasn't about to let her see it. He figured back at the ops center, the others were scrambling to try to make sense of what she'd said. "So, where is the rest of your team?" Grayson asked.

"They're within listening distance."

She held out her hand. Kane removed his earpiece and handed it over. She put it into her ear and said, "Did you get everything?"

"And then some," Thurston replied.

"You know we'll find you all eventually, don't you?"

"You won't have to look too far," Thurston replied.

The room erupted as a flashbang grenade exploded, catching everyone, including Kane, by surprise. His ears rang as he crouched, vision blurred. Through its ear-piercing shriek, he heard automatic weapons fire. Instinctively, he reached behind him and felt for his M17, then brought it around and up. In front of him stood a shooter, one of Basilio's. He had a MAC-10 pointed at Kane, and Reaper knew there was nothing he could do to stop the man from firing.

The would-be shooter's head snapped back as a hole appeared in his forehead. Kane glanced back and saw Arenas standing there in full armor with an HK416 to his shoulder. He glanced at Kane and said, "Come on, *amigo*. Time to earn your pay."

Kane could not hear shit. "What?"

"Work."

"Yeah, I'm good."

"Whatever."

Kane turned and searched for Grayson, but she was nowhere to be seen. No doubt her escort had gotten her out as soon as things kicked off. Basilio was still seated on the lounge with his mistress. He had a hole in his chest and another in his head.

Gunfire filled the nightclub as the team mopped up. It was a good thing the firefight wasn't any larger because Kane was still screwed up from the flashbang.

As quickly as it had begun, it was over.

Thurston appeared beside Kane. "You alright, Reaper?"

"I sure as shit had my bell rung," he growled.

"Sorry about that."

"What the hell are you doing here?"

"Thought you might need backup, so we came along."

"We?"

"Carlos, me, and Teller."

"I had it under control. What about Grayson?"

"She's in the wind."

"Did you hear what she said about Knocker?" Kane asked.

"Yes."

"We have to do something to find him."

"And we will, along with Marek. But right now, we have to get out of here before the police arrive. You good to go?"

"Yes. Where's Reynolds?"

"I'm here."

He turned to see her standing nearby. "You alright?"

"Good to go."

"Then let's get out of here."

CHAPTER 15

Somewhere in South Sudan

The knife bit deep into Knocker's left thigh, and he cried out as pain shot through his every nerve ending. Khazbika wore a tank top and cargo pants. Gone was the indignity Knocker had felt the first time he'd pissed his pants when she'd given him the electric shock treatment. The large set of jumper cables she'd attached to him before doing it had hurt almost as much as the electricity. But that had been four days ago. She'd left him alone to get his strength back before another round.

"Fucking bitch," he cursed, teeth clamped together as he tried to manage the pain.

"You are very strong, Englishman," Khazbika said to him. It was as though she admired his strength.

"How about you bring that pretty neck of yours over here and untie me, and I'll show just how strong I am."

She smiled at him. "In another world, I'm sure we would have made a good team."

"Maybe," Knocker said and tensed as she walked behind him.

He felt the knife pierce the skin just under his shoulder blade. He let out a moan as the pain began radiating outward. Khazbika lowered her mouth next to his ear. "They say that there is very little difference, a fine line, in fact, between pain and pleasure. How does that feel?"

Knocker jerked his head to the side and felt the hard contact of the blow. His torturer reeled back, the knife tip coming free of his skin. Khazbika walked around and stood before him, wiping the blood off her lip. The former SAS man smiled in satisfaction. "You're right. That was quite pleasurable."

"I like you," she said, her eyes glittering.

"Enough to let me loose?"

The knife plunged into his leg. "No."

Knocker screamed.

Worldwide Drug Initiative, El Paso, Texas

"You need to keep your head down, Mary," General Hank Jones growled from the other end of the phone. "The President isn't happy about what happened in Brazil. He has asked the Department of Justice to look into it and put forth their recommendations on whatever action they deem necessary to be taken."

"We did what we had to do, sir. Our job is twofold at present. You might point out that we found out Ellen Grayson is still alive, and we're doing everything we can to track her down. Gustaw Marek has resurfaced too, and we're trying to find him as well. Especially with the fifty-million-dollar price tag he's put on our heads."

"I explained all that, but he's getting grief from Brazil, and there are some things that are under threat if we...*he* is not seen to be doing something about it."

"This is bullshit, sir."

"I agree, Mary, but this is out of my hands."

"Worst case scenario, sir?"

"They could shut you down."

Thurston was taken aback. "After all we've done, sir?"

"It doesn't count for much at this time, Mary. Just keep your head down, and we'll see what happens."

"Yes, sir. Just a heads up. We may need operational clearance within the next few days."

"Where to?"

"I'm not sure. We're trying to nail Marek down."

"Any news on your missing man?"

"No, sir. We gave the admiral all we had on

that, but we are still running our own search in the background."

"All right, Mary. Keep me updated."

"Yes, sir."

The call disconnected and Thurston got up from her desk, rubbing her eyes to relieve the headache that was building. She left her small office and went in search of Ferrero to pass on the good news. She found him in his office, looking through after-action reports. He glanced up and saw the concern on her face. "A penny for them, Mary. You don't look very happy."

"I just got off the phone with Hank Jones. He says the President has the Justice Department investigating the incident in Brazil."

Ferrero placed the piece of paper he'd been reading on the wooden desk. "That sounds like it could be a problem."

"There's talk that we could be shut down."

He stared at her, not knowing what to say.

Thurston continued, "Maybe if I resign, it might make a difference. They obviously need a head to roll, and the buck stops with me."

"No." Ferrero's voice was firm. "You belong here. That is, if you still want to be part of this?"

"Of course, I do."

"Then stay the course, Mary. Ride this bitch all the way down if that's what it takes, but don't give up."

"I'll take it under advisement."

There was a knock on the door, and Swift appeared. "If I'm not interrupting, I have news on both fronts."

Thurston said, "Get everyone back here. To save you repeating yourself, you can tell us all together."

———

"We have news on two fronts," Thurston told her people once they had all settled in the ops room. "I'll let Slick fill you in."

"First point is about Knocker. I can put Grayson and her team in Mosul at the same time. I did a little more digging and came up with this."

The large screen changed, and an ISR feed appeared. They all watched as it showed Knocker being taken and placed into a vehicle before it disappeared. Thurston stared at the tech and asked, "Who the fuck had this hidden away?"

"The NSA."

"Jesus Christ," she swore bitterly. "Get it to Admiral Joseph. I'm guessing he would like an extra-large shit sandwich to chew on. Fuck, those damned assholes. When they were asked, they said they had nothing."

"I'm guessing they know where Knocker is, ma'am, but they aren't saying."

"We'll see. Luis, take over."

"Tread lightly, Mary."

"Lightly be fucked. He's one of ours."

She stormed off, doing her headache no favors. After a moment, Kane asked, "What's going on, Luis?"

"Paper-pusher stuff. Keep going, Slick."

"I've also managed to track down our friend Marek. It was easier since I knew what I was looking for, so I've been able to pick up bits here and there and—"

"Where?" Ferrero interrupted, not wanting to wade through the details of the process he'd used.

"Samokov, Macedonia."

"What do you know?" Kane asked.

"He's holed up outside the village. From what I've seen, he has a security team of around twelve. It looks as though he's paying off the local police, too." Swift brought up a satellite picture of the man's compound, a large estate surrounded by trees and hills. Swift pointed out some features. "You'll see that the estate is surrounded by trees, which will provide you with good cover on your approach. The bad part is, with the hills and trees, there isn't a close LZ or DZ. That means you'll have to go in on foot or—"

"Or drop on target," Cara interjected.

"I vote for that," Axe said.

"Vote for what?" Arenas asked.

"Drop on target. Hit them hard and fast."

The former Mexican Special Forces commander

shook his head. "*Amigo*, sometimes I think you're in too much of a hurry to die. Who is she this time?"

"Why does there have to be a girl?" Axe asked indignantly.

"Because there usually is," Brick said, rolling his eyes.

"Did you get her pregnant?" Teller asked.

"God, I hope not," Axe muttered. "Why? Do you know something?"

"Me? No."

"All right," Kane said. "Let's focus. Axe can tell us about his baby later."

"Shit, don't even go there, Reaper. That's not even a little bit funny."

"You're unbelievable," Reynolds said, frustration in her voice. "You'll charge into a shitstorm of bullets, but when there's a problem with a woman, you run a mile."

"You would too if you met her," Brick told her. "She's got a laugh like a donkey braying."

"Really?" Cara said. "You can't be a little more respectful?"

Kane grinned wryly. "It's true. I thought it was one of those *vuvuzelas* when I first heard her."

"Seriously?"

Kane winced. "Afraid so. I'm starting to think he and Brooke should have stayed together."

"Thanks a lot," Reynolds said. "I got what I needed."

"And you all think *I'm* the bad one in the equation," Axe moaned. "They just use me for my perfect body to fulfill their insatiable needs."

"Oh, please!" Cara face palmed.

"It's all right, honey," Reynolds said sympathetically. "You've got a great body."

"Thanks."

"It's a shame about the wiener," she added with a grin.

Axe opened his mouth to send a retort her way, but he was cut off. "You all done?" Ferrero asked.

They went back to putting their game faces on. It was always the same way after returning from an op. It took them a few days to wind down from the high, but this looked like it would be a quick turnaround.

Slick said, "All right, let me tell you what else I know."

Director of National Intelligence, Washington, DC

"When the fuck were you going to tell me, Brett?" Thurston growled through the phone at the director of National Intelligence.

"Mary?" fifty-year-old Brett Edison blurted, taken by surprise. "What's going on?"

"Your people knew what had happened all along,

and no one said a fucking word."

"Whoa, slow down. Do you know who you're talking to, or have you forgotten?"

"I'm talking to a damned weasel, that's who."

"Careful, Mary."

"Careful, bullshit. I had one of my men taken, and your people screwed us. Take your pants down and bend over. Well, we found out your dirty little secret, and I'm sure once the admiral finds out, he'll be kicking down your damned door."

"I don't know what you're talking about."

"Don't lie, Brett. We found the feed on your servers. It's right—"

"You what?" The director almost exploded through the phone.

"Do I need to repeat myself?"

"You hacked our servers?"

"Not the damned point. The point is you knew my man was taken by Ellen Grayson. How long have you known she was still alive?"

"Need to know, Mary."

"How fucking long, Brett? And more to the point, where the hell did she take him? If you were tracking her, then you know where she took him."

"Mary—"

"Where?"

He sighed. "Khartoum."

Fuck!

"You have to understand, Mary. Your guy wasn't

the objective. The President told us to focus on the bigger prize."

"So he just left Knocker out there to rot on the end of the vine. Then who is the target?"

"I can't say."

"Can't or won't?"

Edison said nothing.

"Shit. Don't worry, Brett, I'll find out for myself."

"Leave it, Mary. This is way above your pay grade."

"Screw you, Brett."

The call disconnected, and Edison stared at the handset before he pressed another button. This had to be stopped before everything they'd been working toward was screwed up.

Thirty minutes later, the door to Edison's office burst open, and not one but two intimidating men strode in. He stared at them and gave them a mirthless smile. "I was expecting you."

"And so you fucking should be," Alex Joseph growled.

Hank Jones walked over to the desk, and for a moment, Edison thought the big man would throw it aside. "When were you going to say something, Brett? Tell me."

"There are only a few people who know, and the President wants it kept that way. My advice to you,

General, is to keep that pit-bull of yours in check."

"Stick your head up your ass and smell what you've been spewing, Brett. We could have had our guy back by now and wrapped up Ellen Grayson as well."

"That's the way the President wanted it," Edison said, wielding the commander-in-chief as though he were a weapon.

"Just what is it you're doing?" Jones asked.

"Need to know."

"Don't give me that horseshit, Edison. My security clearance is top-level. The same goes for Alex. So, what are you doing?"

"We're looking into The Ghost."

"Son of a bitch," Joseph growled. "I ought to come over that desk of yours and bust you in the mouth. We've been running parallel operations, and you kept this quiet. You trying to get a gold star, you selfish son of a bitch?"

Jones stared at him. "You know what, Edison? I'm going to guess the President doesn't even know about this damned operation you're running."

"He does know, and he wants the CIA to keep out of it."

"You jumped-up little punk," Joseph snarled. He took a step forward.

Jones stepped in front of him. "Don't kill him yet, Joe. I still have questions."

"Make it quick."

"Where is he, Brett?"

"Who?"

Jones kept his cool. "The Ghost?"

"We think he's in South Sudan."

"Think?"

"We're not sure."

"Do you know who he is?"

"As far as we know, a former SBS lieutenant named Dan Best."

"How long have you known?"

"A month."

Joseph took another threatening step. "Motherf—"

"Easy, Joe."

"Do you have a team there?"

"Only in Khartoum."

Jones could tell he was lying. "Where, Brett? If I send my people into South Sudan, I don't want them getting shot at by your people."

"You can't send your people in there, Hank. The President won't allow it."

"No one left behind, Brett." Jones turned and started for the door. "Come on, Joe, before I kill him myself."

CHAPTER 16

Biggs Army Airfield, El Paso, Texas

"Once this mission is complete, you're to return home, Mary," Hank Jones stipulated. "Presidential orders."

"You know I can't do that, sir," Thurston replied.

"I didn't think you would."

"By the time we take Marek off the board, I'm hoping we'll know exactly where Knocker is being held."

Jones nodded. "Alex is dispatching Scimitar and his team to look around. Once they confirm a target, then Reaper will be able to join them."

"Here's hoping that Jensen is still alive. After the NSA right royally screwed us, there's a good chance he's already dead."

"Let's hope not," Jones said. "There's a good chance he's still alive. You know these terrorist types like to splash what they do across the internet.

Given that we haven't seen anything yet, well…"

Thurston nodded. "I hope so."

"How's things otherwise?"

"If you're referring to the disciplinary actions I took down in Brazil, I'll say this. The team and I had a robust discussion, and we sorted it out."

"Robust?"

"It got heated for a while, but we're all back on the same page now."

"The joys of command, Mary."

"Yes, sir."

"Make it a good mission."

She looked at him quizzically. "Should I be reading anything into that, Hank?"

"There are people gunning for you, Mary, and I'm afraid that I might not be able to help you this time."

"But you're the chairman—"

She stopped when he spoke over her. "By the end of the week, I won't be. I'm being put out to pasture. It looks like I'm being classified an old dinosaur."

"What happened?"

"Long story and not for you to worry about. Concentrate on the mission."

"What are you going to do?"

"I have something in the wind. I've got an old friend across the Atlantic who has a security firm he wants someone to run an eye over."

"Private sector?" Thurston said, raising an eyebrow.

"Yes."

She held out her hand. "Good luck, sir. And thank you for your ongoing support of our work."

Jones took it, and his face grew grim. "Fair warning, Mary. Be done before I leave."

"I'll do my best, sir."

"Roger that."

Thurston watched him go and turned to find Ferrero waiting. "Is everything alright, Mary?"

She shook her head. "No, Luis. It's far from being all right."

San Marino, Italy

"We may have a location, ma'am," Flint told Grayson. "Not exact, but it is a place to start."

"Where?"

"South Sudan, as we thought. Our team there has identified an HVT associated with the individual they were sent there to find."

"How long before we can deploy Red Team to take the HVT into custody?"

"As soon as we know where he is, a couple of days."

"Good. I'll be joining you when you go."

"What do you wish to do about the other problem?" Flint asked.

"It is only a matter of time before Thurston's people show up on the ground. Deploy Green Team. I want them ready when they do."

"I can have them there by morning."

"Do it. What about the money?"

"It was where he said it was. It was all taken to the secure location."

Grayson nodded. "Thank you."

Flint left her to herself. She walked across to a large plate-glass window and looked at the valley that was spread out before her. This was one of several places she had safe houses, the others being in Johannesburg, Zurich, and Berlin.

Once she had rid herself of the WDI and collected the bounty on The Ghost, she would slip back into the shadows and return the Cabal to life.

Samokov, Macedonia

The night was their friend and the phosphorescence of their NVGs, their lover. Team Reaper made their way down the steep slope of the mountain through the trees with slow precision. They'd been dropped on the opposite side of the high ridge by a Black Hawk helicopter, the landform acting as a buffer for the aircraft's noise. They'd trekked over the top, and their current course would bring them directly down on the compound where Marek was living.

Kane called a halt. "Take five."

They settled down among the tall pines. Kane said into his comms. "Zero Two, copy?"

"Copy, Reaper One," Arenas came back.

"We're at Location Golf. Taking five, over."

"Roger that."

Kane checked the time; it was 01:30. Another two hours, and they would be on target. The team had worked out and agreed on a plan before insertion. After going over satellite photos, they had figured out an optimal position for Cara to set up and provide overwatch with her suppressed .375 caliber CheyTac Intervention sniper rifle, which had a range of two thousand-plus meters.

The others would infiltrate and either take Marek alive or, if he chose to go down the other path, kill him.

Kane's thoughts drifted to the changes that were coming. With Hank Jones being forced out and Thurston under the gun, he wondered what the future might hold for him and his team. Maybe the CIA would take them into the fold, or… Who knew?"

The wind picked up in the trees, and an icy chill touched Kane's exposed skin. An involuntary shiver ran down his spine.

"You alright, Reaper?" Cara asked.

He looked up and saw her standing there, the CheyTac on its sling over her shoulder. "Yeah, I'm alright. Just thinking is all." He didn't mention that he felt like someone had just walked over his grave.

"Get your head back in the game," she said softly. "We can worry about the other later."

He sighed. "You're right. Get them up. We're moving out."

Washington, DC, Minus Five Hours.

Hank Jones walked into Brett Edison's office at 20:30 hours with dread running through his mind. As soon as he saw the smug expression on the man's face, he knew this would be bad. "I'm glad you could come on such short notice, Hank," he said. "I wanted you to be the first to know."

"Know what?"

"Know that once your people return from their current mission, the office of the Worldwide Drug Initiative will be disbanded, and a new office will be formed within the NSA, where a tighter rein can be kept on them."

Jones swallowed the anger he felt rising in his throat. "Really?"

"Yes. I had a discussion with the President, and we both thought it would be the best place for them. Especially with the new intake."

"What new intake?"

"All of the current personnel will be let go and

new ones brought in. We can't have them bringing bad habits into the new team."

"Just like that?" Jones asked.

"I'm afraid so. They'll finish their current mission, however. Nothing happens before then."

"You finally got your way, then."

"What?"

"Come on, Brett. Everyone knows you never liked the team. Now that you've got someone in office who will listen to you, you've gotten what you always wanted. Team Reaper gone."

"It was nothing personal, Hank."

"Bullshit."

"If you say so."

"I do say so. But rest assured, you haven't heard the last of them. I shit you not."

Edison's expression changed and his voice grew bitter. "Just face it, Hank. They're done. Just like you."

"Fuck you, Brett," Jones growled. "You and what you stand for."

———

Skopje, North Macedonia

"I'm sorry if I woke you, Mary, but I have news."

"I wasn't asleep, sir. We've got people downrange. I won't sleep until the mission is done."

"Then I won't keep you long." He went on to fill

her in on the details of his meeting with Edison.

"I see."

"I'm sorry, Mary. I know you put a lot into what you've got. I'll try to fix things, but I can't promise anything."

"I know you'll do your best, Hank."

"Talk soon, Mary."

"Yes, sir."

The call disconnected, and Thurston took off her headset and flung it at the wall in a fit of rage. "Fuck!"

Samokov, Macedonia

"Reaper Two in position." Cara's voice was quiet over the comms.

"Roger that," Kane replied. "Both teams move in."

Kane and Troy broke cover from the trees and reached the low stucco wall that surrounded the compound. They paused for a moment, then Cara said, "Tango down."

They vaulted the wall and kept moving toward the pool house. Kane glanced left and saw Axe and Brick moving toward the tennis court. From there, they would move on the sentry at the gazebo.

"*Hold! Hold! Hold!*" Cara's voice was urgent. All four men dropped to the ground and held their breath. "Brick, you've got two tangos coming at you from behind the tennis court."

"I've got them."

"You take the one on the left, and I'll hit the right."

"Just say the word."

"Three, two, one, execute."

There had been a slight pause in Cara's voice as she fired on two, realizing that if she had fired on her command, her target would have moved reflexively after Brick's bullet had impacted his target. This way, both shots arrived at the same time, and the targets were put down without any hiccups.

"Threat neutralized."

Kane and Troy got to their feet. They moved swiftly and silently to the corner of the pool house. Kane edged around it and saw another sentry standing near the pool. He raised his suppressed 416 and was about to fire when Troy whispered harshly, "Hold."

Kane lowered the weapon and turned to his friend. "What?"

"I saw movement toward the corner of the main house."

"Reaper Two," Kane said. "The corner of the main house. Troy thought he saw something."

"Wait one."

Before she could get back to him, the night erupted with gunfire. Muzzle flashes filled the darkness, and Kane and Troy flung themselves to the ground. Bullets hammered into the side of the pool house above them.

Kane cursed and said, "Cara, put that bastard down."

"Reaper, I can see three shooters and more moving that are trying to flank you."

"Bravo One, give me a sitrep, over."

"We're trying to work it out, Reaper. We're registering heat signatures everywhere."

"Is it a trap?"

"It can't be, but it's sure something."

Kane and Troy returned fire. Meanwhile, Brick and Axe were trying to flank the immediate threat. "Keep them pinned, Reaper, while Brick and I flank them."

"Yeah, real good, Axe," Kane growled as he fired a burst at a muzzle flash. "I'll do what I can."

The firing grew more intense, then the call came over the radio, "Taking fire. Troops in contact."

It was Axe. Things were going south rapidly, and if they weren't careful, they would take casualties, and that would be it.

———

The CheyTac slammed into Cara's shoulder, and through the night scope, she saw another target go down. Things were fast getting out of hand, and she knew the others were relying on her to get the job done. She worked the bolt and ejected the spent cartridge. The fresh round went home, and she quickly found another target.

Once more, the rifle bucked, and a shooter died. She said, "Reaper Four, passage is cleared. Proceed."

"Copy."

Cara shifted her aim back to the house, where Kane and Troy were still taking incoming fire. She saw that one of the shooters was on the ground, but two more were firing at a steady rate.

She worked the bolt again and squeezed the trigger—another one down. "Hang on, Reaper, one more to go."

"Reaper Two, we're picking up heat signatures moving in from the east. Confirm."

The call had come from Teller, Reynolds' second seat. Cara panned right with the rifle and picked up the movement. She stopped and waited for the pattern to become clearer. When it did, she muttered a curse. "Reaper Two to all call signs. We've got visitors coming in from the east. From what I can see, they're pros."

Cara fired. One of the shooters fell, and the rest scrambled for cover.

"Reaper Two, numbers, over," came the call from Kane.

"One less than before. Estimate ten to twelve."

"Copy."

Another shot, another kill.

Cara cursed again. "Zero, requesting air support.

We need to drop something on these pricks before they can reorganize and cause all kinds of issues."

"Roger, Reaper Two. We're on it."

Cara then reached out to Kane. "Reaper, I've just called for air support. Dig in and hang on."

"Copy, Reaper Two. Digging in."

Skopje, North Macedonia

Ferrero looked at Reynolds. "You're cleared hot, Brooke. Give our people some cover."

"Roger that." She worked the joystick and brought the Gray Eagle around for a safer run. Out of the corner of her mouth, she said to Teller, "Talk to me."

"I've got targets in three different positions, the largest group being to the east."

"Let's light them up."

"Ready when you are, Mama."

"Don't turn me on that way, Daddy."

Teller chuckled. "Just fire the damn missile."

"Missile gone."

Ferrero watched the screen until the missile impacted the target. Then he heard Teller say, "We have target impact."

Samokov, Macedonia

Cara's night sight flared at the impact of the missile, and the valley was rocked by the explosion. She closed her eyes until the flare died, then went back to work. "Reaper, you're clear."

"Copy, Reaper Two. Moving."

Kane fired twice and dropped another shooter as he hurried past the pool. The missile strike had stopped the concentrated fire from the east, which made their passage easier. He reached the corner of the house and followed the garden along the side until he got to the next corner. There he waited for Troy, then moved toward the main entrance.

On the gravel turn-around were three dark SUVs, and he suddenly realized who the extra shooters were; they were from Grayson. She knew they'd come after Marek, and she'd placed men there to be ready—except they'd had an up-close and personal encounter with a Hellfire. But it didn't mean—

The door of the main entrance opened, and something flew toward them. "Shit, get down."

The grenade exploded in a bright flash, and Kane felt the heat of it wash over him. Gravel rained down on the two team operators like hailstones. "You all right, Troy?"

"Still in the fight. Reaper."

Kane came to his knees as a handful of shooters spilled out of the open doorway. With a flick of his finger, he switched the rate of fire on his 416 to auto and lit them up. Behind him, Troy did the same, and the shooters performed the macabre dance of the dying under the assault of the incoming rounds.

The two Team Reaper operators pressed forward, stepping over the bodies in the doorway. They raised their NVGs as they entered the brightly lit foyer. Troy was first in, and he swept it from left to right.

Kane followed him in and moved right toward a closed door. Troy walked backward toward him, watching their rear and the door on the left. He put his back against the wall near the doorframe and looked at Kane. He gave a nod, and Kane let his carbine hang by its strap and drew his M17. He opened the door and walked through.

———————

Axe and Brick entered through the rear. After dealing with the two shooters outside on the paved dining area, they gained access and cleared the kitchen. It was empty, so Brick led the way into a large dining hall. The table was long and ran almost the full length of the room. As Axe went down one side, Brick traversed the other. They met at the opposite end and moved into a hallway. They reached the foyer just as Kane and Troy breached the room on the left.

Gunfire erupted from within the room. Axe took a couple of steps toward the door, but the door on the right opened and an armed man appeared, wielding an automatic weapon.

The 416 in Axe's hands spat fire and the man was thrown back against the doorframe before sliding down it slowly, the weapon spilling to the floor. Without interrupting his pace, Axe changed direction and entered a spacious room.

The man on the other side of the doorway held a handgun at shoulder height, ready to shoot, and as soon as Axe appeared, he squeezed the trigger. The big man grunted from the bullet strike, and he staggered for a moment before falling to his knees. Behind him, Brick's suppressed 416 rattled off three shots, the casings clinking and skittering across the tiled floor.

The shooter fell and rolled onto his back. Brick hurried forward to check the threat and found it had been neutralized. He checked the face of the man against a picture he had taped to his forearm and saw that it was Marek himself. He pressed his transmit button on his comms and said, "Reaper Five to all call signs. Jackpot. I say again, Jackpot."

He turned away from the dead Marek and hurried to check on Axe, who was still on his knees. "How you doing, old man?"

"It fucking hurts," he groaned.

"Where'd he get you?"

"Body armor. Think he broke a fucking rib."

Brick slapped him on the back. "You'll be all right."

"Thanks. Great of you to check, old cock."

The former SEAL grinned at his use of one of Knocker's favorite sayings. "Can you get up?"

"Yeah, just give me a minute to catch my breath."

Kane and Troy appeared in the doorway. Kane looked at his friend. "What's wrong?"

"Took a round to his chest plate. He'll live."

"Good, then get him up. We're out of here. Cara, how are we looking outside?"

"All clear so far."

"Right, we're coming out. Mission accomplished."

CHAPTER 17

Juba, South Sudan

Former SEAL Chief Borden Hunt watched the two men across the street from where he and Rucker sat in their old, battered VW van. They'd been parked there for an hour and were no closer to finding out if these were the two men they needed to follow, or they'd been barking up the wrong tree for the better part of the afternoon.

"This is bullshit," Rucker growled as he ran his hand through his light-brown hair in frustration. "The admiral has sent us on a Hail Mary assignment here, Bord."

"Maybe," Hunt said. "But we'll nevertheless see it through."

Both men worked for Joseph's Special Activities Division. Four of them had been deployed to South Sudan, Hunt, Rucker, Grady Taylor, and Molly Hollister. Taylor and Hollister were back at their safe house. They monitored the comms and were hooked into a satellite feed, one that would go blind in— Hunt looked at his watch—twenty more minutes.

"Scimitar, copy?" The voice came through his comms.

"Copy, Grady."

"Coming along the street is an old Toyota Landcruiser. Molly and I have seen it go past twice already. It might be worth keeping an eye on."

Hunt looked out the window as it drove past. "I'm on it."

The vehicle slowed down, and he could see there were two men inside. Then it stopped, blocking their view of the men they were watching. There was movement, then the Toyota drove away.

"They're gone," Rucker said.

"Yeah. Follow that Toyota," Hunt said. Then, "Grady, our targets just got into that Toyota. Stay with it as long as you can."

"We've got it covered."

Rucker started the VW and grated the gears as he engaged first. They pulled onto the street and began tailing the Toyota.

———

They drove through the narrow streets of Juba until the Toyota turned right and passed a makeshift checkpoint made of old tires and barbed wire blockades. Standing sentry were three men armed with AK-47s.

"Keep going," Hunt said, pointing across the street. "Then pull up over there."

Rucker did as he was ordered, then cut the engine. Hunt climbed into the back of the van and pulled the curtain aside far enough to see out the back. He said, "Molly, have you still got the Toyota?"

"Sure have, Bord, but our window is about skunked. Two minutes tops."

"Tell me what you see."

"They're driving along the street. This part of Juba is known for its unsavory types. Armed militia has taken root in there. It's a good haven for terrorists who pay them for protection."

"So, the guy we're looking for could be in there?"

"It's possible."

"And we're about to run out of fucking time," Hunt muttered.

"It looks like they're pulling up outside a building, Bord. We might be able to get something before we go offline in the next thirty seconds."

"Here's hoping."

"Someone has come out to meet them. He's struggling...and we've lost the feed."

"Shit. Send me what you've got to look at," Hunt said and grabbed the Toughbook from beside him. "Ruck, keep an eye open."

Hunt waited for the screen to come to life, then skipped through the pictures that had been captured until he came to the last one. He zoomed in as best he could and looked at the figure. Molly said, "Just before we lost the feed, when the guy came out, he looked like he was struggling on crutches."

Hunt concentrated on the man. He flicked through a couple more pictures until he got to the last one, where the man, for some reason, looked skyward. "Got you."

He turned to Rucker. "Time to go home."

———

"We got him, ma'am," Flint said into the encrypted satellite phone. "In Juba, South Sudan."

"Good. I'm glad since everything else has turned to shit," Grayson hissed.

"What happened?"

"Marek is dead, and the team we sent to Macedonia was wiped out. Fucking bastards."

"The WDI?"

"Yes. Who else?"

"What do you want to do?"

"Forget about them for the moment. We need to concentrate on our terrorist friend. He's worth fifty million dollars to us. With that, we can get the Cabal back to where it was."

"Did you reach out to the others?"

"Yes. My people have been working to put a new council together. They have convinced the members from France, Germany, Belgium, Italy, and Greece to come on board."

"Some of the biggest armies in the EU."

"Yes, and we will need to stand together against the aggressors of the communist east."

"Why not America?"

"Maybe once we are established, but not quite yet. Not after what happened."

"And the UK?"

"That is still a work in progress," Grayson allowed.

"I will have Red Team in-country inside a couple of days. You will be with them?"

"I said I was going to be."

"Then I will talk to Miller and work things out."

"I'll see you then."

"Yes, ma'am."

———

Skopje, North Macedonia

"All right, get it all packed up as quick as you can," Thurston barked. "We need to relocate as soon as possible."

Word had come through from Alex Joseph that there was a possibility the man they were seeking was in Juba, South Sudan, so the team was in the process of packing up everything and getting ready to move.

"Reaper, a word," she called to her team commander.

Kane and the others had been back for all of ten hours, seven of which had been downtime while they slept off the op. "Yes, ma'am?"

"Once we relocate, I want you, Cara, and Carlos to go over a plan of attack. Let the rest of the team run their eyes over it in case they can see something you missed. Remember, this place is a hotbed."

"We'll work the problem, General."

"You can forget the rank. I've received word that I'm being discharged from the military, and as of tomorrow, I will be a civilian. Everyone else is being let go as well."

"So, what is it we're doing?"

"Getting to Africa as fast as we can before Uncle Sam comes knocking. Knocker is our first priority, and I'm still in command until tomorrow. So, fuck them."

"Yes, ma'am."

Suddenly the door to the operations center opened. The center was inside a large warehouse that was able to house all their equipment with ease.

Walking in were four men dressed in suits, and they had "spook" written all over them. Their leader was a man Thurston knew on sight. "What do you want, Brett? You're a long way from home."

"I'm here to shut you down."

"We're not shut down until tomorrow," Thurston stated.

"Yeah, well, since you've wrapped up your op here, you're all done."

"No, we're not done until tomorrow."

Edison reached into his pocket and took out a piece of paper. He unfolded it and passed it to Thurston. By this time, the rest of the team had gathered around then. Kane glared at Edison. "What the fuck are you doing?"

"I'm here to speak to your boss, not you."

Kane looked at Thurston. "What's happening?"

"According to this, we've been disbanded."

A murmur ran through the team. Cara said, "Is there something you need to tell us, ma'am?"

Thurston stared at Edison and felt like ramming the smug look on his face down his throat. "This asshole has talked the President into bringing the WDI into the National Intelligence fold under new command and new operators. We're all out of a job."

"We've still got a mission to complete," Axe said. "Knocker is still out there."

"Not your problem anymore," Edison told him.

"But we have a lead."

"I can't help that."

"Can't General Jones do something, ma'am?" Axe asked.

"The general is no longer in a position of power." The expression on Edison's face grew even smugger.

"Permission to punch him in the face, ma'am?" Axe asked.

"Stand down," Thurston ordered, but she had drawn her sidearm. Before the National Intelligence man realized what was happening, the barrel of the M17 was placed against his forehead. "All right, this is how things are going to work. Take their weapons and tie them up. We've got a man downrange who needs to come home. We're going to get him."

"You'll get locked up for this."

"Yeah? Oh, well. It'll be worth it."

Minutes later, they were all tied up while the rest of the team completed their task. Once they were done, Thurston walked over to Edison. "I'll have someone come and untie you after we're gone."

"And I'll have someone come and arrest you once we're untied."

"Asshole."

On her way out the door, Thurston picked up her encrypted satellite phone and dialed a number.

"Jones."

"We have a problem."

"Tell me about it."

Thurston went into detail about Edison. There was a sigh from the other end. "Get your man back, Mary. I'll see what I can do. Just don't be too keen on getting back to the States for a while."

"I kind of expected that, sir. But there is another problem there as well."

"Families?"

"Yes, sir."

"It may take a few days, but I'll see what I can organize there as well."

"Thank you, sir."

Juba, South Sudan

"What do we have, Bord?" Thurston asked the former SEAL.

Hunt stabbed a finger at the map on the table. "We believe they are holding him here."

"Are you sure?"

"No, ma'am," he said with a shake of his head. "That's one thing we're not sure of. However, we did get this picture." Hunt put the picture on top of the map.

Kane leaned over and stared down. "Is that him?"

"We believe it is The Ghost, yes. If he's here, Knocker could be here too."

"What's the terrain like?" Kane asked.

"The neighborhood is like Syria on a Saturday night. It's full of terrorists and small fry wanting to make a name for themselves. Going in there is going to be hairy at best."

"Well, we're going in; that's a no-brainer," Thurston said. "How the team gets back out is up to them."

"It's going to be tricky without air support," Kane pointed out.

"Darkness is your friend, Reaper. Use it, get the job done. Work out a plan and bring it to me."

"Yes, ma'am."

Thurston left Hunt and Kane to look over the map. The Team Reaper commander looked at his counterpart and said, "I could use a good satellite picture about now."

Hunt took a pen and circled a point on the map.

"This is the target building." Another circle. "Over here is a building that allows a good field of fire down this street and this one. Put Cara in there with one of my people to watch her back, and she can provide overwatch. The rest of us can take the building."

"That all sounds fine, but I can tell by your voice that it's not going to be that easy."

"We've counted about twenty men around the target building alone," Hunt told him. "Throw in the others that are all around the neighborhood, and you've got an estimated sixty or seventy fighting-aged males who want to do nothing more than to kill Americans."

"Should be interesting, then."

"Might I suggest we break into two teams?"

"Tell me, Bord. Let's work it out."

"There is no working it out," Hunt replied. "We have to get in there and back out as quickly as possible. If we get caught in there, we're all fucked. We won't have the firepower to get out. It'll be Mogadishu all over again, except there will be way fewer of us than there were with them."

Kane nodded slowly. "You're right. Without air support, we're as screwed as a New York hooker giving out freebies on a Saturday night."

"What are we going to do?" Hunt asked.

"There's only one thing for it. Get air support."

"But where?"

"The last place you'd expect it."

—————

"What?" Thurston blurted. "You never thought to run this past me before you made the decision?"

"It was the only decision to be made, General," Kane said. "Besides, they were already here on a separate mission."

"How do you know that?"

"I just do."

"Shit."

"The visitors are here," Cara called.

"Make a decision, ma'am," Kane said. "They can help us with manpower and air support."

"Fine. Let them in."

Two men came into the makeshift ops center and

stopped in the center of the room. One was a tall man with broad shoulders, a buzz-cut, and tattoos on his arms. The other was shorter but just as wide as his companion. Kane stepped in front of the big man and held out his right hand. "Grigory, it is good to see you. Thanks for coming."

"You did not think I would come?" the Russian mercenary asked. "I have not forgotten about our debt. Now it is time to repay it."

Kane stepped aside and introduced the man to Thurston. "Grigory, this is General Mary Thurston. She's my boss."

"It is good to meet you. Now you are our boss too. This is Adrik Grekov. He is my lieutenant. The others are outside."

"Others?" Thurston inquired.

Baburin glanced at the gathering crowd of operators and nodded sharply. "Yes. I have ten more men."

The general nodded. "Reaper said you had air?"

"I have an MI-24. It can be used to insert men at the target and fly air cover for a time."

Thurston stared uncertainly at Baburin for a long time before saying, "Alright. Get with Reaper and make a plan. We go tonight."

Baburin smiled broadly. "I like her, John. She could be my next wife."

Kane winced and waited for the expected explosion. Instead, Thurston rolled her eyes and said, "Men and their fucking testosterone."

Kane took Baburin and Grekov aside and showed them a map. Hunt and Cara came to join them. "This is the target building, Grigory."

The Russian made a grim face. "Hmm, this is not good. This whole area has plenty of bad men."

"Have you ever been in there before?"

Grekov grunted. "Once. We lost four men in there. It was a mistake we said we would never make again."

"What is so important in there, anyway?" Baburin asked.

"Two things. We have a man in there and the HVT who is holding him."

"Who is HVT?"

"The Ghost."

The big Russian smiled. "Fuck me, you have found the grail of the terrorist world right under our noses."

"You in?"

"Hell, yes. What do you want us to do?"

"There is a roadblock here," Kane said, pointing at the map. "I'll take my team in the vehicles with some of your shooters. You take the rest of your team on the helicopter. Cara will go with you. I want her in this building here. Can you give her support?"

"Yes. I will have one of my men stay there with her."

"Thanks, Grigory."

"I will go and organize things for tonight. It promises to be good, yes?"

"It promises to be something."

Best sat opposite Knocker, with Khazbika standing behind him. For the past couple of days, she had left him to recover his strength before another round of torture began. The former SAS man was tired; the combination of pain and lack of sleep saw to that. However, he was still determined to outlast whatever they threw at him—except death, of course. If they chose to kill him, there wasn't much he could do about it. So far, most of it had been superficial, designed to inflict maximum pain without killing him.

"I have word that your friends are looking for you," Best said. "They must like you a lot. More than my friends did."

"People looked for you."

"One of them found me and couldn't even follow a simple instruction. You weak cock."

"I tried to get people to come back for you, but the bitch wouldn't do it. The funny part is, she was the one who delivered me to you."

"What?" Best looked confused.

"Grayson. The woman you paid for me. She was the one in charge of the operation. *She* was the one who wouldn't help me get you out."

"You're a liar."

"Really? She was the head of MI6 special operations. She's had more people killed and run more ops than you've had hot dinners, chum. Fucked up there, didn't you?"

Knocker could see the tremble in Best's lip as anger surged through him. "You paid ten million to the woman who could have fucking saved you. Hahaha."

"Khazbika!" Best roared. "I want to leave."

He sounded like a spoiled child.

Khazbika helped him to his feet and said to the guards, "Lock him back up. I will play with him later."

Knocker was untied and dragged back to the small room where they kept him. In the corner was a stinking bucket he used for defecation. Flies buzzed around it, and with the heat now radiating inside the room, the stench would become unbearable.

He laid down on the hard floor and stared at the stained ceiling. From what he'd picked up from the guards talking, he was in Juba, South Sudan. If he could escape before becoming too weak, he knew where the SIS had a safe house. It wasn't his first time in-country.

Knocker ran different things through his mind to try to keep it sharp. His body hurt from the various wounds, and his right eye was partially closed from a blow he'd received from one of the guards.

The door opened, and Khazbika filled the doorway. Her nose wrinkled at the smell of the enclosed space. "Get up and come with me."

Knocker dragged his tired frame erect and stood

in the center of the room. He lurched across toward the door with the sudden realization that he might never be able to escape from this place. His strength was mostly gone.

He followed her down a hall and into a room that resembled a kitchen. Their route had taken them past a staircase that led upward. Khazbika pulled out a chair and said, "Sit."

The former SAS man sat down. She tossed a stale loaf of bread on the dirty table. "Eat."

Knocker's hands reached across the space, and he grabbed it in his claw-like fingers. He put it to his open mouth and his teeth ripped into it, tearing a large piece free. His jaw ached as he chewed the tough morsel before swallowing.

"It tastes like shit," he growled, taking another bite.

"I am happy you are enjoying it."

There was movement at the doorway, and a man appeared. He spoke with an English accent. "It is ready."

"What?" Knocker asked suspiciously.

"A bath."

The former SAS man cocked an eyebrow. "What?"

"Come," Khazbika said.

Getting up from the chair, wincing with pain, Knocker lurched after her. She took him to a room with a long tin bath in it. "There."

Knocker walked over to it and leaned down. He

tested the water with a grimy finger, and it was hot. Khazbika turned to the armed escort. "Leave us."

"But—"

"Go."

She turned back to Knocker and walked over to him. He tensed involuntarily, half-expecting the knife to plunge into his body. Instead, Khazbika said, "Let me help you."

She started to undress him, starting with his filthy shirt. Instead of resisting, Knocker let her do it. Soon he was naked, his squalid clothes thrown into a corner. His body was covered with bruises and dark patches of dried blood where his wounds had crusted over.

"Get in the bath."

Knocker climbed in, the hot water prickling his skin and feeling good. After sitting down, he leaned against the hard rim and closed his eyes. He felt Khazbika washing him with a rag she'd picked up from beside the tub. She started to hum softly, and the former SAS man found it disconcertingly soothing. "Why are you doing this?" he asked.

"It was ordered."

She washed his chest, her hand moving in lazy circles.

"Is this, like, a last rites kind of thing?" Knocker asked. "Clean me up before you kill me?"

Khazbika said nothing. She just kept washing him, slowly working lower until she reached his groin. Knocker tensed as the rag ran across it, then moaned as he felt himself respond. The former SAS man cursed himself under his breath.

The motion of the rag stopped. Khazbika let it go, and it sank deep into the water. She ran her fingers lightly across Knocker's abdomen until she reached his hard member. Slender fingers wrapped around it and she fondled it, making him even harder.

"Shit," Knocker groaned.

"Would you like me to stop?" Khazbika asked.

"No point in stopping something you've already started," Knocker replied. "It might be the last time old Knocker gets the pleasure of female company."

She leaned forward and kissed him.

_____

Khazbika had joined Knocker in the bath. She faced away from him as their gyrations slopped water from the bath onto the floor. Her head was thrown back, her face tilted toward the stained ceiling. Cries of passion escaped her lips and joined the former SAS man's animalistic grunts.

Knocker reached out and grasped her hips, feeling his end quickly approaching. They peaked together, their cries echoing around the room.

They collapsed together, Khazbika slumping onto Knocker's chest, her right arm hanging over the side of the bath. Their breathing sounded loud in the enclosed room.

"Do you kill me now like a praying mantis?" Knocker asked.

It was the second time he'd asked her, and once again, she failed to answer him. Knocker reached over her shoulder with his left hand, running it down her chest so it cupped her breast. His thumb flicked her hardened rose-colored nipple and it stiffened. Then, like a coiled rattler, she moved to strike.

Khazbika's right hand came up with her knife. It was stopped by Knocker's right hand, which he locked onto her wrist, stopping it from moving any farther.

The former SAS man's left arm wrapped around the lethal woman's slender neck and started to squeeze. Khazbika realized she'd made a deadly mistake by assuming her prisoner was unprepared for her strike. His arm tightened, and panic surged through her body as she felt the unbelievable pressure constricting the life from her.

Khazbika started to thrash, her legs kicking violently, water splashing on the floor. She clawed at his arm with her left hand, nails raking grooves in Knocker's skin.

He whispered in her ear, "Don't fight it. Your time is now."

With one forceful movement, Knocker broke her neck. She slumped against him, and the knife fell from her grasp.

He had to struggle out from beneath her and was almost out of the tub when a sound came to him—the low *whop-whop-whop* of an approaching helicopter. "Man, I hope that's what I think it is. If it isn't, Knocker, we're fucked."

CHAPTER 18

Juba, South Sudan

"Red Bear One is on target," Baburin's voice came through loud and clear.

"This is Reaper One. We're thirty seconds out."

Cara heard both calls as she worked her way toward her target building. In front of her was Grekov, armed with the new model AK-12, while behind them, the helicopter lifted off.

Grekov crashed through the front door and was met by an armed Sudanese man. The Russian fired twice, and the man fell to the floor.

Moving through the building with a smooth efficiency until he found the stairs, he indicated for Cara to go up while he watched her back. Farther down the hallway, another shooter appeared. Grekov switched the fire selector and squeezed the trigger. A three-round burst erupted from the weapon's muzzle and stitched the shooter's chest.

Shouts erupted from the room the man had emerged from. Grekov retrieved one of his RGN fragmentation grenades and pulled the pin, tossed it into the room, and took cover.

The explosion was deafening.

He moved back along the hallway and went up the stairs to the room where Cara had set up. She looked at him and said, "You made enough noise."

The Russian shrugged with a smile. "It was necessary."

"Just watch our backs."

Grekov grunted.

Cara said, "Reaper Two in position."

"Copy, Reaper Two. Reaper One arriving on target now."

After taking care of the roadblock at the entry to the neighborhood, Kane's team had split up upon reaching the target building. He and Troy, along with two of the Russian operators, took the front of the building, while the other vehicle that held Axe, Brick, Traynor, and Arenas went to the rear. The Russian mercenaries under the command of Baburin took up security positions at each of the four intersections.

As soon as Kane and the others exited their vehicles, a handful of men appeared from the building, firing at the intruders. Bullets hammered the side of the vehicle like hail peppering a corrugated iron roof. The noise was terrible, and the number of incoming rounds forced the four men to take cover. Troy popped up from behind the engine block and fired a burst from his 416.

Two of the shooters jerked and spilled to the ground, their weapons silent. Troy dropped back down and said, "We need to get in there now."

Kane took a fragmentation grenade from his webbing, pulled the pin, and threw it toward the doorway. "Frag out!"

———

Knocker had started to put his foul clothes back on when the first rattle of gunfire reached out. He spun to face the door as it was flung open by an armed guard, his face a mask of panic. Knocker's arm rose and fell, his right hand releasing the knife. The weapon tumbled over and over before burying itself in the chest of the guard.

Knocker hurried forward and scooped up the man's AK-47, then relieved him of his spare magazines. He straightened and moved to the doorway, shirtless and shoeless, only his pants covering him.

An explosion sounded from outside, mixed with the heavy gunfire. Knocker ignored it. He had only one thing in mind: to find Best and complete the mission.

The hall was vacant as he started down it. He went to the room where they'd tortured him and found it vacant. From there, he began a methodical check of each room. Unfortunately, Best was nowhere to be seen.

By now, firing was coming from the front and the back of the building. Shouts of alarm were followed by an explosion. A terrorist appeared on the stairs that led up to the second floor, and Knocker fired from instinct and muscle memory. Three rounds from the AK hammered into the man's chest, and he went down hard.

Knocker hurried forward and grabbed the man by the shirt, then shook him. "Where is Best?"

The terrorist looked up at the Brit. He smiled, and blood ran from the corner of his mouth. "Fuck you."

The accent, though made thick by the blood, was American. "Shit," Knocker said, shoving the dying man back. "These guys are a fucking mixed bag of sweets."

Knocker was about to start up the stairs when the door to his right moved. He swung the AK around and depressed the trigger. The weapon roared, and bullets punched through the thin wood, splintering it. A cry of pain told him all he needed to know.

The Brit moved over to the door and pulled it open. A shooter lay dead on a set of stairs that went down into a dark abyss. A muzzle flashed, and bullets flew past Knocker's head. He threw himself back and landed on the floor, pain shooting through him. He half-sat up and flicked the fire selector of the AK to full auto, then squeezed the trigger. The Kalashnikov rattled until the magazine ran dry. Knocker then reloaded and climbed to his feet, taking cover beside the doorjamb.

Another burst of fire sounded from down the stairway, followed by frantic shouts. They didn't want him down there for some reason, and he could guess what that was. They were covering for Best, giving him time to get away. Knocker figured there was a tunnel down there somewhere the terrorist was using to make his escape.

Knocker leaned in and fired a long burst with the AK. A cry of pain erupted from below, but so did another storm of gunfire. Bullets chewed deep into the wall opposite the doorway. A shout from behind the Brit caused him to spin around. He was a hair away from firing and killing the man he teased the most on the team—Axe.

"Don't do that, you fucking tosser. I almost killed you," Knocker growled.

"Knocker?" Axe said.

"Yeah, it's me. I know I'm not a pretty picture, but—" More gunfire rang out from the building's basement. "You got a fucking grenade?"

"You know me. I always have a grenade," Axe told

him with a grin. Looking Knocker over, he asked, "You sure you're alright? You look like shit."

"I'm not ready to fall down yet," Knocker lied. "Now, put a fucking grenade down there, will you?"

Axe pressed his transmit button. "Reaper, you need to get your ass in here. I've got Knocker."

"Be right there."

"Brick, I'm in the hallway. I need you, buddy."

"Give me a damned grenade, Axe," Knocker growled. "The bastard is getting away."

"Who?"

"The Ghost, who do you think? Mary-fucking-Poppins? Put it down there."

Axe took a grenade from his webbing and pulled the pin, then tossed it down the stairs and called, "Frag out!"

The explosion rocked the inside of the building, and dust and debris belched from the doorway. Knocker looked at Axe. "Give me your NVGs."

"What?"

"Give me your NVGs. Hurry up; we're wasting time. I don't have any, and it's dark down there."

"Shit, Knocker," Axe growled, taking off his ballistic helmet with his NVGs attached.

Knocker put it on and lowered the night vision optics.

"Hey, what are you doing?" Brick shouted as he came into the hallway.

"Doing something I should have done years ago,"

the Brit said and entered the stairwell.

Brick followed him down. It was hard to see through all the dust in the air. Knocker made out three bodies on the floor. One had taken the brunt of the blast from the grenade and was missing a leg.

The Brit peered around, and he made out the hole in the wall opposite. "That way."

The two operators started into the tunnel. Brick's comms came to life. "Reaper Five, where are you?"

"We found a tunnel below the house, Reaper. Could be our HVT is using it to escape."

"You need to get out of there. We've got tangos closing on our position."

"Knocker, we've got to go," Brick said in a low voice.

"Bullshit, we do," he cursed. "That bastard is being taken off the board."

"Reaper, we're Charlie Mike down here."

Brick could imagine the look on Kane's face at the news they were continuing their mission, and the image wasn't pretty. He waited for a moment, then heard Kane say, "Reaper One to all call signs. Dig in. Cara, you're in charge. Brick, Troy and I are coming to you."

CHAPTER 19

Juba, South Sudan

"What the hell is going on?" Ellen Grayson asked, seeing and hearing her opportunity to snatch The Ghost disintegrate. "Talk to me."

"Someone has beaten us to it," Flint growled. "They're hitting the target house."

"Who, damn it?"

"I don't know."

"It's them," she hissed. "It has to be. Close in and finish them off."

"This isn't the time or place," Flint argued. "Our lookouts are reporting that the shooting is attracting unwanted attention."

"Damn them," Grayson hissed. "Get us out of here. Tell the team to pull back. With some luck, the locals will do what I couldn't."

She stood listening to the automatic gunfire and

the explosions while Flint made the call to the team. From the background, Miller stepped forward. "Ma'am, it's time to go."

She turned and looked at him. A curt nod gave him his answer. "All right. Call the others in."

"Knocker, stop," Kane said in a harsh whisper.

"I'll stop when I'm dead, Reaper. This bastard needs killing. I should have done it the first time I saw him."

"What do you mean?"

"I ran across him in Mosul years ago on an op for SIS. I'll tell you about it when we're done."

The tunnel went straight for around fifty meters, and the direction it traveled indicated they were under the street. Aware that there could be hidden IEDs in the tunnel, their progress was slow.

The tunnel turned to their left and ran for another twenty meters before stopping at an opening. On the other side was a T-junction.

"Which way now?" Kane muttered.

"Fuck," Knocker hissed. "This way. He turned right and kept going."

Kane noticed that the big Brit was limping and shone a flashlight at his feet. Both were bloody from lacerations.

"Knocker, your feet," Kane said.

"What about them?"

"They're bleeding."

"I'll worry about it later."

Kane grabbed him by the shoulder. Knocker spun and lashed out, swiping the hand away. "Fuck off, Reaper. I'm seeing this through. Go back if you want, but I'm not leaving it unfinished. There's two people in this world I'm going to kill before I'm done. Best is one, and that bitch is another."

"Grayson?"

"Who fucking else? You coming, or what?"

"All right. Just, let me take point."

Knocker stepped aside and waved him past. "Be my guest."

They kept moving until the tunnel reached the basement of another house. Kane had started to ease his way through the opening when gunfire erupted from the other side. He hissed as a round sliced through his clothing and opened a gash in his left upper arm, then lurched back and let out a curse.

Troy stepped forward and filled the void, opening up with his 416. The weapon was on auto, and he sprayed the room beyond with a full magazine.

The shooter on the other side went silent, and Troy took cover to reload while Brick moved through the opening, brushing Knocker aside. He swept the basement and said, "Clear."

The others followed him through, Kane's arm already starting to throb. Brick had reached the stairs and was beginning to ascend the rickety treads to the main part of the building. Once he reached the top, he almost walked into another ambush. He jumped back as bullets peppered the wall around the doorway. He said aloud, "I think these guys are trying to stop us from doing our job."

"I've had about enough of those fucking wankers," Knocker snarled and stepped through the doorway.

"Knocker, wait!" Kane called after him, but it was too late. Gunfire erupted, and the hallway filled with muzzle flashes. "Shit."

"Hold it there, Nutter, before I knock you ass-over-tit," Knocker shouted, his voice echoing along the street. He'd killed the shooter in the hallway and gone outside, guessing that Best would have a vehicle close by.

Best was hobbling away on his crutches, armed guards on either side of him. Both men spun to open fire, but the former SAS man beat the one on the left to the punch. The AK spewed bullets, and the man fell at the disabled feet of his master. The second shooter, however, was about to fire, and Knocker still hadn't gotten his own weapon into line.

A suppressed 416 let loose and the second shooter fell. Troy stepped up beside Knocker and said,

"You're welcome, buddy."

The Brit glanced sideways at him. "Who the fuck are you?"

"Your new best friend."

Knocker grunted and turned his attention to Best, who had staggered around to face him. Kane and Brick fell in beside him and Troy. The terrorist put his arms out and said laconically, "I guess this is it."

Knocker was suddenly aware of how cold the night air was as it pricked the skin of his exposed back. He grunted. "I guess it is," he said and squeezed the trigger.

The former SAS man moved forward and stood over the dead terrorist, then looked down at him and shook his head. "The poor prick never stood a chance."

"You knew him?" Kane asked.

"Yeah, in a different life."

"Well, we'll be joining him in his new one if we don't get out of here now," Brick said.

Kane nodded and said into his comms. "Reaper Two, sitrep?"

"We can still get out of here if we move now, Reaper. ISR is showing tangos moving in from the east and north."

"All right, get everyone to the vehicles. Have the helicopter stay overhead until we're moving. We'll be right with you."

"Roger that."

"Bravo, copy?"

"Read you Lima Charlie, Reaper One."

"We've secured Reaper Three and the HVT is down, over."

"Good work, Reaper One. Come on home."

"Roger that. Reaper One, out."

————————

"Hey sweetheart, how's it hanging?" Cara greeted Knocker as she hugged him.

"Nothing a couple of beers won't fix," he replied tiredly.

"I'll buy you one just as soon as we get back."

"All right, ma'am, you can let him go now," Brick said and wrapped an emergency blanket around Knocker. "I need to get an IV line into him before we leave."

"I'll do it," Rucker said. "You just keep checking him over."

"We don't have much time," Hunt pointed out.

"It won't take long. It's just to rehydrate him."

"I'm fine," Knocker grumbled.

"I'll be the judge of that."

"Him a tough cookie, huh?" Baburin said.

Knocker turned his head to look at the Russian. "A sod goes away for a short time, and it all goes to shit. Now you're letting Russians join the team."

"He's funny, too."

The Brit winced as the IV needle was inserted. "Shit a brick, you're trying to kill me."

"Stop your crying and suck it up, Princess."

Kane stopped what he was doing and listened to the message coming over his comms. He looked up and said, "That's it, we've got to go. The door is closing."

They got Knocker into the back of the second Humvee with Brick so the medic could finish going over him. Arenas said to Kane, "The other Humvee is cooked, *amigo*."

"Put a charge in it. Are the other vehicles good?"

"Yes."

"Let's do it."

Two minutes later, the team was mobile and headed back to their base, all present and accounted for.

"How is he?" Thurston asked Doctor Rosanna Morales.

"He'll be just fine. I will need to keep an eye on his feet and make sure they don't become infected. Someone took care of the knife wounds."

"Knife wounds?"

"Yes, they stabbed him and then kept them clean so they would partially heal, then they did it again. He's been beaten as well, and at some point, he lost a tooth. But for the most part, it was a knife. I've got some IV antibiotics running into him, as well as another bag of saline. He's been put through the wringer, and I have no doubt he's hurting, but you wouldn't know it. He doesn't let it show."

"It's an operator thing. Is it all right if I talk to him?"

"Sure, but I think he's gone to sleep."

"I would be if you two ladies would have your meeting somewhere else," Knocker growled.

Rosanna shrugged. "He's all yours."

Thurston walked over to the cot and looked down at the Brit. He opened his partially closed eyes and said, "Now that's a face a man could get used to waking up to."

"I'm glad to see they didn't dent your sense of humor, Raymond."

"They tried, ma'am."

Thurston nodded. "I'm sorry we didn't find you sooner."

"Not your fault."

"Kane said you knew him. The Ghost."

"Lieutenant Dan Best. Former SBS. I came across him on a mission in Mosul years ago. Went missing in Somalia."

"What happened?"

"He had been crippled by his captors. He asked me to kill him. I couldn't. I wanted to get him out, but Grayson told me to leave him. Along the way,

I picked up a foreign fighter. He was British. She told me to kill him, but I thought the intel he could give us would be valuable. I was about to put him on the chopper when one of the others put a bullet in him. On her orders."

"And she took you off the street in Mosul?"

"Yes. I owe her for that. As soon as I'm upright and we're back in El Paso, I'm going to find her."

Thurston looked concerned. "About that…"

Thurston never got any farther since the commotion that erupted in the main area drew her attention. "Shit, what now?"

———

Edison had found them, and this time, he'd come with a team of black-ops specialists. Six men held their weapons on the team in case of trouble. The National Intelligence commander smiled callously. "You're all going to prison. Be thankful it isn't one here."

"What for?" Axe asked.

"Disobeying a Presidential order, for starters."

"I didn't hear him give it."

"It came from me."

"Yeah, but you can tell us any old shit, and how would we know that it's true? Besides, you aren't in our chain of command."

"Chain of command?"

"Yeah. Thurston, Jones, and then the President. Fuck off."

Kane tensed.

"What?" Edison blurted.

Thurston said, "He's right. That's the chain of command. We do not take orders from you."

"You do now since I'm taking over."

"We are being disbanded and replaced, right?" Thurston asked.

"As of right now."

"So we're civilians?"

"Yes."

"Then you have no authority over us. Fuck off."

Edison waved one of his men forward. "Arrest her. She'll do for a start."

The room filled with shouting and chaos as weapons came clear of holsters and were pointed in all directions. The situation was one step away from becoming a bloodbath. That was when a dark-haired man wearing a suit entered the room.

"Put the weapons away!" he shouted, silencing the room. He had a British accent. "Allow me to settle this once and for all."

"Who are you?" Edison snarled.

"Noah Bancroft, MI6."

"What do you want?"

Bancroft reached into his pocket and took out a piece of paper. "I'm here to stop you from causing a major international incident."

"What?" Edison looked confused.

"The piece of paper I have here explains it all. But in case you can't read, old chap, it says that everyone here is a citizen of Great Britain, and they are in this country doing the work of Her Royal Majesty's Government."

Axe chuckled. "I knew I loved that old girl."

Edison snatched the paper from the SIS officer. "This is horseshit."

Bancroft winked at Thurston, who smiled at him in return. He said, "In case you're thinking about saying what the hell and ignoring that piece of paper, I have a team of SAS specialists outside, waiting to transport these British citizens back to their home country."

Kane saw Edison's face grow darker with rage the farther he read. He looked up, screwing the paper into a tight ball. "You won't get away with this. The United States government will do everything in its power to put you all behind bars, and I will be out front leading the charge."

"You come after us and expect to get spanked, Edison," Kane said to him. "As you already know, we're not that easy to apprehend."

"There will come a time when no one will be able to help you. Any of you. And when it does, I'll be there waiting."

"Have a nice day, Mister Edison."

With a wave of his hand, Edison and the others

left. Thurston turned to Bancroft. "What is going on?"

"Like I said, you're all officially citizens of the UK."

"How? What?"

"Hank Jones. He's going to work for the Global Corporation, a private contracting firm owned by George Peacock the Third. The government uses his people for different things across the globe. Hank Jones reached out to him, he pulled some strings, and here I am. One thing about Peacock. If you work for him, he'll back you all the way, provided you operate within the bounds of the law."

"What will we be doing?"

"Exactly what you have been doing but with a view to change. England is having a surge in drug importation right now, but there will come a time when you might be required to do other things such as personal protection details or hostage rescue in countries where British military need to be kept clear."

Thurston looked at Kane, who couldn't quite believe what he was hearing. Cara stepped forward and said, "What about my son? Kane's sister? Carlos' wife and children?"

"Anyone with family they care for or live with is automatically covered," Bancroft replied. "Your son is now a British citizen as well."

Thurston turned to her people. "All right, it's up to you. The choice is yours. I know some of you have families, but you also heard what Edison said. If any of us go back to the US, he'll try to lock you up."

Arenas stepped forward. "You will need to get my family."

"Only have to make a call, old chap."

"I will go."

"Me too," said Axe. "Can you get me a meeting with the queen?"

Bancroft smiled. "I'll see what I can do."

One by one, the team came forward and agreed. The only ones left were Kane, Cara, and Ferrero.

Kane said, "We'll all be together?"

"Yes."

"Luis?"

"I don't see we have any choice."

"Cara?"

"I go where you go, Reaper."

"Then I guess we're going to England."

"I'll arrange transport," Bancroft told them.

Thurston nodded. "All right, everyone, listen up. Get all your personal effects together and leave the rest behind. If it doesn't belong to us, it stays."

Hunt said, "It's been a pleasure working with you, ma'am."

"You too, Bord. Say hi to Alex for me."

"Yes, ma'am."

Kane slapped him on the shoulder. "If I ever need help, Bord, I'll—"

"Just holler, Reaper. We won't be far away."

The two men shook hands. "Luck, Bord."

"Luck, Reaper."

An hour later, the team was on a military Airbus A400M Atlas C1 transport to England and a new chapter in the lives of Team Reaper.

———————

RAF Brize Norton, Oxfordshire, England

Hank Jones was waiting for them when they got off the transport. Beside him stood a thin man of around fifty with a balding head and tired-looking eyes. He wore a suit under a knee-length coat that kept out the cool breeze.

Thurston, Ferrero, and Kane walked over to them while the others mingled off to one side. "Good to see you, sir," Thurston said to Jones.

"You too, Mary. I hear you had a successful mission."

"One less terrorist in the world, sir, and we got Knocker back. Can't go home, though."

"Their loss is my gain, I believe," the man beside Jones told her.

"Mary, this is George Peacock, the owner of the Global Corporation."

"Pleased to meet you, sir."

"George will be fine. If we're working together, I think first names are appropriate."

"Thanks for getting us out of a tight spot, George."

"Thank Hank. He was the one who convinced me I couldn't do without you, and it seems he was right. I'd lost three men trying to find that terrorist."

"You, sir?"

"Yes, the government outsourced the intelligence gathering on him. They came to my company to help out."

Thurston nodded. "Sir, this is Luis Ferrero. He's my second in command. And John Kane, the team commander."

"Gentlemen, pleased to meet you."

"You too," Kane said.

"And the rest of your team."

"Good people, every one of them, sir."

"Fine, fine. We are based out of Hereford—"

"Just fucking wonderful."

They all looked at Knocker, who was being wheeled across the tarmac by Morales in a wheelchair. "Good Lord," Peacock muttered.

"How are you, Colonel?"

"Jensen."

"Great, they know each other," Jones grumbled.

"Don't tell me, you're involved in all this, right?"

"You might say that. How have you been?"

"How the fuck do you think?" Knocker growled. "I get taken off a street in Mosul, sold to a terrorist I could have prevented from becoming one years ago, and got tortured by a crazy cow with a bloody knife in South Sudan. Killed that fucker, though."

"So, it's about the same."

"Yes, sir."

Thurston gave Knocker a questioning look. "The colonel was my commander in the SAS for a while."

"Say no more."

"No, ma'am, it's not like that. We played nice together, right, Colonel?"

"One of my best," Peacock agreed.

"So, you're contracting now?"

"Still working for Her Majesty."

"Great to see you again, sir."

"You too, Knocker."

Rosanna wheeled him over to the others. Peacock turned to Thurston. "Once you arrive in Hereford, you'll be assigned quarters on our base. We're on the opposite side to 22 SAS Squadron base. I'll leave you with Hank, and he'll give you the rest of your orders. I'll be seeing you soon after you all settle in. Make a list of what you need, from weapons to toilet paper."

"Yes, sir."

Peacock left them, and Thurston said to Jones, "Thank you for all you did, sir."

Jones nodded. "This is a new beginning for us all, Mary. I'm hoping that it'll work out. After you get settled, come and see me tomorrow, and we'll talk."

"There's still one more mission to complete, sir," Kane said.

Jones nodded. "I know, Gunny. I know."

CHAPTER 20

The café was small and out of the way, surrounded by the desert-colored stucco buildings that lined the alley. Seven round tables sat outside on the cobblestone street. Only one was occupied. The woman in the sunglasses and wide-brimmed sun hat sipped her tea in the early morning sun.

A butterfly floated down and landed on the edge of the table, its wings slowly pulsing as it thought about taking flight. Then it lifted off and flew away, disturbed by the approach of a man coming along the alley.

Grayson stared at him for a moment, but the bearded face was unfamiliar. When the man drew close enough, he changed direction and sat down opposite her. "You really shouldn't go out on your own," Knocker said to her. "You never know who you might meet. And don't become a creature of habit."

Grayson placed the cup on the tabletop as she moved her opposite hand beneath the table. "Leave the gun where it is, Ellen. I've got a Beretta pointed at you."

She sighed and raised her hands, resting them on the table. "So, what now? You kill me? Is that it?"

"Maybe."

"You don't have the stomach for it, Raymond," she said, her voice filled with sarcasm. "If you did, you would have been able to do as you were ordered years ago."

"I've come a long way since then."

Grayson picked up her cup of tea and took a sip, then replaced it. A voice came to Knocker through his earpiece. "She's triggered a silent alarm. You've got three minutes tops."

Knocker stared at her. "You know we've got your money, right?"

"You're lying," Grayson said smoothly.

"Seized your electronic funds and found the millions in cash you took from Alfredo Costa."

Grayson stiffened. "You're lying."

"You know me better than that, Ellen. I have no reason to lie."

Her face twisted into a mask of rage. Knocker smiled. "There she is; the bitch is back. What now for your Cabal?"

"They will never be gone," she hissed. "They will always be there in the shadows, waiting to come out at the right time."

"Two minutes, Knocker."

She shrugged. "I hear that you and the others aren't welcome at home any longer."

"Is Edison one of you?" the Brit asked.

"We are many."

Knocker nodded. "The thing about the many is that they seem to be becoming fewer."

"There will always be a Cabal. Who else will watch over the world? Watch over the Chinese, the Russians, the Middle East minority groups that seek to wreak terror on the world? We weed out the weak and—"

"All you do is line your own pockets with money," Knocker interrupted. "You claim to be watching over the world. Protecting it from bad people on both sides of the spectrum. But in fact, the only people you give two shits about are your own kind. And when that doesn't work out, you kill them off and start again. You shouldn't be called the Cabal. You're like a phoenix. You keep rising from the ashes. Well, guess what? From now on, whenever and wherever you all stick up your heads, old Knocker is going to be there to kick the fucking shit out of it."

"You can't stop—"

The sound of the suppressed Beretta could

be heard from beneath the table. Ellen Grayson jerked under the impact of the round. Her eyes widened and she opened her mouth, trying to speak. Blood flowed from the corner, and her head lolled forward.

Knocker climbed out of his seat and tucked the Beretta into his waistband before casually walking away.

"One minute, Knocker."

"Job's done. So is the Cabal."

––––––––––––

National Security Agency, Fort Meade, Maryland

"Sir, I've got something you should take a look at," the thin-haired, bespectacled man said to Edison from the doorway to his office.

Edison glanced up from his paperwork. "What is it, Henry?"

The man called Henry walked forward. In his hands, he held a laptop computer. He placed it in front of Edison. "This came off the main server thirty minutes ago."

"What am I looking at?" Edison asked.

"Just watch, sir. You'll see."

Edison watched. It was feed showing a woman sitting at a table. "Where is this?"

"Bucharest, sir."

A man entered the picture and sat down. The angle of the feed didn't show the man's face. The man and the woman talked, and things turned nasty when the man shot her.

Edison sat back and looked at Henry. "He just killed her. Am I right in saying that?"

"Yes, sir?"

"And we don't know who the man was?"

"No, sir."

"The woman?"

"We made her as former MI6. Ellen Grayson. She was supposed to be dead."

Edison nodded. "Leave it with me, Henry."

"Yes, sir."

"Close the door on your way out."

He waited until Henry had gone and the door closed before he took out the second of his cell phones. This one was encrypted and untraceable. He punched in a number and waited for the person on the other end to answer. When it was picked up, he said three words.

"Nemesis is dead."

_____

Hereford, United Kingdom

Kane lay on his back in the middle of the extra-wide double bed. Cara lay with him, her head resting on his chest. Knocker had arrived back in Hereford earlier that morning, his mission complete, and hopefully with it, the death of the Cabal. But as Kane well knew, it might only prove to be a deterrent for a short time. Or maybe they would go back to living in the shadows. Wherever they went, he hoped never to hear from them again.

"How's Jimmy?" Kane asked Cara.

"He's good. I've told him where I'd be if he needed me. He's old enough to be left alone. Besides, who's going to try anything on this base?"

"It must be good to have him with you now."

"It is. I guess that it is the one plus to come out of this whole shitty deal."

Kane thought of his sister still in the States.

"Are you alright?" Cara asked.

"Yeah, I'm fine."

She ran a hand across his chest until it reached one of his nipples. She gave it a sharp squeeze.

"Ouch, shit. The damn well hurt."

He rolled on top of her and dug his fingers into her ribs. Cara let out a yelp, followed by a giggle. "Get off me—"

The cell on the table beside the bed rang. Kane buried his head in the junction of Cara's neck and shoulder. "Fuck."

"Answer it, Reaper. I'm not going anywhere."

He crawled over to the edge of the bed and reached for the phone. He picked up the cell and hit the answer key. "Yeah?"

Kane listened for a moment. "No, haven't had the television on all day."

More listening, then he disconnected. He looked at Cara. "Three bombs have gone off in London. It's time to go to work."

A LOOK AT: DEADLY WATER BY BRENT TOWNS AND SAM TOWNS

A car bomb in a quiet suburban street sets in motion an investigation which will uncover the tentacles of organized crime stretching from the water-starved outback to the halls of power in the country's capital.

Senator Colin Worth was about to introduce a water bill which would cost the big producers millions before he was assassinated. However, the trail—as investigated by Detective Sergeant Gloria Browning and her team—only throws up more questions than answers.

Meanwhile, former undercover operative Dave Nash is brought in to investigate the disappearance of a water inspector in the town of Collari, on the Barwon River. But things take an even darker turn when Gloria's daughter, Rachel, is abducted.

Now, to get her back, Nash has to go against an organization who feeds its victims to the trees.

ABOUT THE AUTHOR

A relative newcomer to the world of writing, Brent Towns self-published his first book, a western, in 2015. Last Stand in Sanctuary took him two years to write. His first hardcover book, a Black Horse Western, was published the following year. Since then, he has written a further 26 western stories, including some in collaboration with British western author, Ben Bridges.

He has written the novelization to the upcoming 2019 movie from One-Eyed Horse Productions, titled, Bill Tilghman and the Outlaws. Not bad for an Australian author, he thinks.

He says, "The obvious next step for me was to venture into the world of men's action/adventure/thriller stories. Thus, Team Reaper was born."

Brent lives in a country town in Queensland, Australia with his wife and son.

CPSIA information can be obtained
at www.ICGtesting.com
Printed in the USA
LVHW032051310521
688957LV00007B/1395